Early English Women Writers 1660–1800

Early English Women Writers 1660–1800

ELIZA HAYWOOD

THREE NOVELLAS

The Distress'd Orphan
The City Jilt
The Double Marriage

Edited with Introduction and Notes
by Earla A. Wilputte

MICHIGAN STATE UNIVERSITY PRESS
EAST LANSING

Early English Women Writers 1660-1800: No. 5

ISBN 0-87013-428-0
Copyright 1995 by Earla A. Wilputte

All Michigan State University Press books are produced on paper
which meets the requirements of American National Standard of
Information Sciences—Permanence of paper for materials
ANSI Z23.48-1984.

Michigan State University Press
East Lansing, Michigan 48823-5202

A Colleagues Book Series
editor Robert Uphaus

Published originally by
Colleagues Press in 1995.

CONTENTS

ACKNOWLEDGMENTS

I wish to express my gratitude for assistance received from the Thomas Fisher Rare Books Library and the John Robarts Research Library of University of Toronto. In addition, I would like to thank librarians Barbara Phillips, Marilyn MacDonald and Angela Hagar at the Angus L. MacDonald Library of Saint Francis Xavier University and Nancy Minard and Karen Smith of Killam Memorial Library's Special Collections at Dalhousie University. I have also been assisted in many valuable ways by Jamie Powell, Marie Gillis, W. J. Howard (University of Toronto), David Oakleaf (University of Calgary) and my parents, Ruth and Earle Wilputte.

INTRODUCTION

I

LITTLE IS KNOWN about the personal life of Eliza Haywood. What was once believed to be fact has been thrown into doubt by recent scholarship. George Whicher, in his *Life and Romances of Mrs. Eliza Haywood* (1915), presented what has, until lately, become accepted as truth: she was born Elizabeth Fowler, daughter to a London shopkeeper, about 1693; she married a clergyman, the Rev. Valentine Haywood and bore him a son, Charles, in 1711; and in 1721, Haywood put an advertisement in *The Post Boy* declaring that his wife had eloped and that he was no longer responsible for her debts.

Recently, two undated letters signed by Eliza Haywood have been discovered, one corroborating that her maiden name was, indeed, Fowler. Both letters seek patronage for publications — one for a "Tragedy" lately performed (probably her first, *The Fair Captive*, 1721), the other for her translation of *La Belle Assemblée* (1724). The letters are important for the light they shed on her marriage; however, they do not provide clear information. The first letter refers to her "unfortunate marriage" that reduced her to the "melancholly necessity of depending on my Pen for the support of myself and two Children, the eldest of whom is no more than 7 years of age." The other letter refers to "the Sudden Deaths of both a Father, and a Husband, at an age when I was little prepar'd to stem the tide of Ill fortune."[1] The first letter still suggests an unhappy, abandoned marriage; while the second letter's reference to her dead husband may be a euphemism for a husband who is dead to her. There is no record of a second child born to Eliza and Valentine Haywood, leading us to believe either that she is lying (as Charles would be ten, not "7 years of age" in 1721) or that she had illegitimate children since leaving her husband.

In 1715, Eliza Haywood was acting on stage in Dublin's

[1]Cited in Gabrielle Firmager, "Eliza Haywood: Some Further Light on Her Background?" *Notes and Queries* 38 (1991): 181–182.

1

Smock-Alley in Shadwell's *Timon of Athens*, a profession she returned to in 1730. In 1719 she wrote the phenomenally successful novel *Love in Excess; or, The Fatal Enquiry* and embarked on a writing career that would span nearly four decades and include plays, poems, translations, novellas, periodicals and novels as well as stints as an actress and publisher.

Eliza Haywood died on February 25, 1756 and was buried in St. Margaret's churchyard, next to Westminster Abbey. The graveyard has since been grassed over—nothing now shows where Haywood rests.

II

For too long, Eliza Haywood has been known to modern readers only as the first prize in the pissing contest in Alexander Pope's *Dunciad*, Book II:

> See in the circle next, Eliza plac'd,
> Two babes of love close clinging to her waist;
> Fair as before her works she stands confess'd,
> In flow'rs and pearls by bounteous Kirkall dress'd.
> The Goddess then: "Who best can send on high
> The salient spout, far-streaming to the sky;
> His be yon Juno of majestic size,
> With cow-like udders, and with ox-like eyes."
>
> (II.ii.157–166)[2]

Pope portrayed Haywood, one of the most successful and prolific authors of the first half of the eighteenth century, as an object whose purpose, like the china chamber pot which is second prize in the contest, is to be filled up by men. Pope condemned Haywood as a passive, docile, sexually promiscuous dunce. Damning by omission, he attacked her on the basis of her sex, not her authorship. His reference to her "Two babes of

[2]Alexander Pope, *The Dunciad*, James Sutherland, ed., *The Twickenham Edition of the Poems of Alexander Pope* (London and New Haven, 1963), 5: 303.

Love" is effectively ambiguous. It accuses her of having bastard children, and thus sullies any reputation of her being an honourable woman, while it also personifies her two scandal novels with which Pope was personally incensed. For Pope, Haywood as woman and author was capable only of illegitimate, second-rate productions, be they human or literary. She figures in *The Dunciad* as a type of the Goddess — an irresponsible, prolific matrix of dullness. Pope's friend and fellow Scriblerian, Jonathan Swift, referred to Haywood in his correspondence of October 26, 1731 as "that stupid, infamous, scribbling Woman."[3] Obviously, Eliza Haywood must have been a literary force to be reckoned with to elicit such violent responses.

She was a dangerous entity in the eighteenth century: a writing woman, writing for women. Haywood, like many female authors before her, was labelled and condemned by men as unfeminine, licentious, immodest and usurping. She dared to wield that masculine instrument, the pen, and speak her mind in public like a man. Her novels, which carried such titillating titles as *Love in Excess*, *The Mercenary Lover* and *The Fatal Secret, or, Constancy in Distress*, detailed erotic scenes of passion and pornography such as this seduction from the *Adventures of Eovaai* (1736):

> [He] snatch'd her to his Breast, printed unnumbered Kisses on her Lips, then held her off to feast his Eyes upon her yielding Charms: . . . his eager Hands were Seconds to his Sight, and travell'd over all; while she, in gentle Sighs and faultering Accents, confessed she received a Pleasure not inferior to that she gave.[4]

or this rape from *Idalia: Or, The Unfortunate Mistress* (1723):

---

[3]Cited in *The Dunciad*, Sutherland, ed. (London and New Haven, 1963), 5: 443.

[4]*Adventures of Eovaai, Princess of Ijaveo*, Josephine Grieder, intro. (New York and London, 1972), 48–49.

. . . she felt the Clothes thrown off, and something catch
fast hold of her. . . . What was now the Distraction of this
unhappy Lady, waked from her Dream of Vanity to certain Ruin! unavoidable Destruction! She rav'd, she tore,
did all that Woman could, but all in vain! — In the midst
of Shrieks and Tremblings, Cries, Curses, Swoonings, the
impatient *Ferdinand* perpetrated his Intent, and finish'd
her Undoing.[5]

A quick survey of the verbs employed in these two passages
reveals part of Haywood's political point: the man actively
"snatch'd," "held," "feast[ed]" and "travell'd" while the woman is
described in the passive as "yielding" and "faultering" until,
finally, she "confessed" her pleasure. The seduction becomes a
kind of torture to enforce female submission to the man. In the
second passage cited above, even though the woman, in her
resistance, is much more active, the "impatient" rapist "perpetrated" and "finish'd" his intent through sheer superior force.

Eliza Haywood did not offer mere gratuitous sex and feminine fantasy; she had an important moral and social message to
convey through her exhilarating tales. Often in her novels, the
sexual encounters are interrupted, and it is the consequences of
the illicit liaisons that are explored rather than the sensual expe-
riences themselves. James Sterling points out in his dedicatory
verse to the third edition of Haywood's *Secret Histories, Novels,
and Poems* (1732):

You sit like Heav'n's bright Minister on High,
Command the throbbing Breast and watry Eye,
And, as our captive Spirits ebb and flow,
Smile at the Tempests you have rais'd below:
. . .
The tender Maid here learns Man's various Wiles,
Rash Youth, hence dread the Wanton's venal Smiles —

[5]*Masquerade Novels of Eliza Haywood*, Mary Anne Schofield, intro. (Delmar,
N.Y., 1986), 16–17.

. . .

> Born to delight as to reform the Age,
> She paints Example thro' the shining Page.[6]

Sterling praised Haywood as the "Arbitress of Passion" and, along with Aphra Behn and Delariviere Manley, one of the "fair Triumvirate of Wit."[7] The poem describes Haywood's narrative strategy as involving her readers' emotions so that she can better teach them how the passions can override reason even in a controlled setting like reading.

Haywood's first novel, *Love in Excess; or, The Fatal Enquiry* (1719), along with Defoe's *Robinson Crusoe* and Swift's *Gulliver's Travels*, was "the most popular fiction of the eighteenth century before *Pamela*."[8] Her works, at least sixty-seven titles, appealed to a wide audience and attempted to describe for women the dangers posed to them by men and a masculine world. Today, we would call Haywood a feminist; in his verse, Sterling called her "the Proxy of vindictive Heav'n!" — a champion of innocence.

Haywood's early novels, though, are far from innocent, and she often attached moralistic dedications to them in defence of her steamy style. The purpose in writing erotic works like *Lasselia, or the Self-Abandoned* (1723), she explained, is

> only to remind the unthinking Part of the World, how dangerous it is to give way to Passion, [which] will, I hope, excuse the too great Warmth, which may perhaps, appear in some particular Pages; for without the Expression being invigorated in some measure Proportionate to

---

[6]Cited in John Richetti, *Popular Fiction before Richardson: Narrative Patterns 1700–1739* (Oxford, 1969), 181.

[7]*Ibid.*, 181.

[8]William H. McBurney, "Mrs. Penelope Aubin and the Eighteenth-Century English Novel," *Huntington Library Quarterly* 20 (1957): 250.

the Subject, 'twould be impossible for a Reader to be sensible how far it touches him. . . .[9]

It was her intention to draw her readers into the passionate world of her imperiled heroines — always on the verge of rape, imprisonment, illicit love — in order to teach them that every woman is subject to this kind of treatment and is often powerless to prevent it. Haywood, as narrator, would often speak directly to her audience to involve them not only in emotionally experiencing passion through vicarious adventures but to engage their reason. In *The City Jilt*, Haywood writes:

> Some perhaps, into whose hands this little Narrative may fall, may have shar'd the same Fate with poor *Glicera*; like her have been betrayed by the undoing Artifices of deluding Men; like her have been abandoned by the Perfidy of an ungrateful Lover to Shame, to late Repentance, and neverending Griefs; and it is those only, who can conceive what 'twas she suffered, or know to compassionate the labouring Anguish of a Heart abus'd and inspir'd in this superlative degree. The happy *Insensible*, or the *untempted* Fair, are little capable of judging her Distress, and will be apt to say her *Misfortune* was no more than what her *Folly* merited: yet let those pitiless Deriders of her Frailty take care to fortify their Minds with *Virtue*, or they will but vainly depend on the Force of their own Resolution to defend them from the same Fate she mourn'd.

Unwilling to be identified with the "*Insensible*" prude or the "untempted" and therefore undesirable woman, Haywood's female reader must associate herself with the undone, abandoned, suffering heroine who has been wronged by "deluding

[9]Eliza Haywood, "To the Right Honourable the Earl of Suffolk and Bindon," cited in *Women in the Eighteenth Century: Constructions of Femininity*, Vivien Jones, ed. (New York, 1990), 153.

Men" and her own honest heart. Every good woman is a potential victim, warns Haywood, and she must sympathize with the fallen ones and fortify her mind against deceptive men and her own frail heart to prevent her own ruin.

Haywood's goal in these novels is to evoke a "moral-emotional sympathetic vibration rather than a self-conscious and deliberate assent to moral ideas."[10] The narrative patterns entrap the virtuous heroine and make her powerless against the evil machinations of men (which are often reinforced by the legal system and social practice). With few exceptions, the narratives lead to the heroine's death, retreat to a convent or decision to retire from the world of men. The three short, amatory novels presented in this edition exemplify Haywood's vision of the virtuous woman falling prey to the avaricious appetite of men and her own excessive capacity to love.

III

Eliza Haywood's writing career can be divided into two distinct periods and corresponding genres: the amatory novels of the 1720s and '30s, and the moralistic, didactic works of the 1740s and '50s. The two-part structure of her career is definitely related to Pope's placement of her in his *Dunciad* (1729). Finding Haywood guilty of satirizing his friends Martha Blount and Lady Henrietta Howard in two of her scandal novels — *Memoirs of a Certain Island adjacent to the Kingdom of Utopia* (1725–26) and *The Secret History of the Present Intrigues of the Court of Caramania* (1727) — Pope essentially ruined Haywood's reputation as an author. To Pope, Haywood was just another hack — a writer who supported herself through a prodigious outpouring of poor, amateur scribblings. After her appearance in *The Dunciad*, Haywood was silent for almost a decade. When she did publish, she did so anonymously. She returned to acting and worked for a

[10]Richetti, 182.

time with Henry Fielding's Great Mogul's Company until the Licensing Act of 1737 severely curtailed the theatre.

With the success of Richardson's *Pamela; or, Virtue Rewarded* in 1740, Haywood realized that tastes in literature were changing and that she must change with the times. She began to write conduct books instructing servant maids, husbands and wives how to behave; she started up three different periodicals: *The Female Spectator* (a feminine version of Addison and Steele's very popular paper) (1744–46), *The Parrot* (1746), and *The Young Lady* (1756), each offering advice, moral and practical, on how to conduct oneself in society; and she turned her hand to the new kind of novel — realistic, even domestic in detail, sentimental and moralizing. *The History of Miss Betsy Thoughtless* (1751) is the most popular of Haywood's later works, but *The Fortunate Foundlings* (1744) and *The History of Jemmy and Jenny Jessamy* (1752) were also successful.

Haywood's new style was hailed as a moral conversion, a fallen woman with a sordid past having learned the value of virtue and morality. However, more than anything, Haywood's explicitly didactic style demonstrates her business acumen. The medium had changed, but not the message. The fragrant gardens, panting breasts and trembling lips of the 1720s were no longer acceptable in the 1750s, but Haywood still aimed to warn her readers about the social injustices to women: the need for better education for women, a wife's right to leave an abusive husband, the wrongness of the sexual double standard, and the falseness of men.

Haywood's obituary in *The Whitehall Evening Post* (for 24 February to 26 February 1756) recognized her as "the celebrated Authoress of some of the best moral and entertaining Pieces that have been published for these many Years,"[11] ignoring entirely the erotic novels of her early career that are equally moral and perhaps even more entertaining.

---

[11]Cited in Gabrielle Firmager, "Introduction," *The Female Spectator* (London, 1993), 5.

IV

The three novellas presented here — *The Distress'd Orphan*, *The City Jilt*, and *The Double Marriage* — were published separately in 1726 but were originally intended for a single volume. They did appear together in the first of a two-volume set, Haywood's collected *Secret Histories, Novels and Poems* (1727) with *Letters from the Palace of Fame* and *The Lady Philosopher's Stone*, a translation from the French. They are arranged here chronologically — they were published in January, June and August respectively of 1726; when read sequentially, they manifest a darkening vision of the relationship between Man and Woman.

The plots of these amatory novellas, like most of Haywood's early stories, threaten their heroines with seduction, rape, enforced marriage, the mad-house, and death. As fantastical as these events sound when listed together, each was a possible fate for an eighteenth-century woman. Arranged marriage, though fading in popularity, was still practiced by enterprising parents and friends; losing one's virginity to a false lover could result in the loss of reputation and a consequent social death; and refusal to adhere to the male-dominated society's rules of behaviour could lead to a woman's confinement by her family or husband in her own home or in a private mad-house. Haywood's early novels, though containing an element of escapism, illustrate the very real social evils threatening women.

In each of these stories, Haywood emphasizes the liminality of the female in masculine society. The heroine's name in *The Distress'd Orphan*, Annilia, comes from the Latin *nihil*, *nil* or "nothing," which describes her legal and social status as woman and orphan. Haywood makes her point even more explicit by drawing the parallel between wives and lunatics in English law: Annilia's guardian "had the same Pretensions to her Estate while [she was] suppos'd a lunatick, as his Son would if made her Husband." In *The City Jilt*, when Glicera is seduced by her lover's false words, she finds herself pregnant and subject to "Shame, Reproach, and never-ending Woe," while her seducer turns his back on her and marries an heiress. Finally, Alathia is socially undone by the bigamous Bellcour in *The Double Marriage*. She commits suicide to release her husband from his original vows and to "deliver [him] from the upbraidings of an injur'd, but too tenderly loving Wife."

Haywood illustrates in these three novels different ways in which women are imprisoned — be it literally in a mad-house as Annilia is, figuratively within a rigid social and moral code as Glicera is, or by the caprice of men as Alathia is. Haywood's point in employing the prison motif is that all women in eighteenth-century society are fettered, in thrall to their own emotions and bodies, but also subjugated to men's desires and greater physical and social power. Those females who attempt to escape their man-made prisons are either punished or allowed only a fraudulent freedom, such as Annilia's. Having been freed from the mad-house, she demands her estate from her guardian and immediately hands over all of it to her new husband. The narrator comments that Annilia's action confirmed her husband's good opinion of her. Annilia's chains are softer now, but she is still not free.

Glicera and Alathia assert themselves in different ways — Glicera attempting to avenge herself on men by behaving like them, Alathia disguising herself as a man to find out the truth about her husband — but both remain imprisoned. Glicera turns from the world of men and isolates herself in her home, her own prison, while Alathia, in judgment of herself, commits suicide with a man's sword. There is no happily-ever-after for women in this society, Haywood states; only one kind of prison is exchanged for another.

Haywood's plots continually make clear that women have much to be angry about: the sexual double standard; the justice system's refusal to recognize a woman's "very being or legal existence" in marriage; the social effacement of woman's identity; and the paradoxical insistence that woman is too childish to assume practical responsibilities but is morally responsible for herself and her partner or family. Through her stories, Haywood allows women a catharsis, a socially acceptable outlet for their anger.

But while her heroines are victimized by men throughout these tales, Haywood also infuses them with strength, courage and conviction which allow them, for a time, to rise above or avenge their ill-usage. The reader is constantly reminded that women are morally superior to men even if lacking in social and personal power. Annilia possesses "a Strength of Mind, and an unshaken Constancy, infinitely beyond what could be expected from her Years, or indeed what we have many Examples of in the other Sex." She manages to marry her true-love, expose her villainous guardian and, hopes the narrator, "meet with a Recompence proportion'd to [her] Merit." Once abandoned by her lover, Glicera turns jilt—one who leads men on and then discards them—and uses one man against another to the ruin of both. Vindictive and emotionally aloof with her beaux, Glicera is nonetheless portrayed as an avenging angel for fallen women but also as a monster created by men—a prototype of Lillo's anti-heroine, Millwood, in *The London Merchant* (1731).

For the most part, men are presented as the enemy in these works, as Haywood stresses the notion of gender-based polarities: Woman, loving, constant and honest versus lecherous, betraying, inconstant Man. Haywood's literary treatment of men is particularly heavy-handed in order to make her didactic point. She is, as we have seen, writing a kind of morality drama, and so the characters must be generalized rather than realistic. In fact, Haywood's male characters are often based on stock stage characters: the lecherous old man who preys on young women; the trusted guardian/uncle who assaults his ward; and the authoritarian patriarch who insists on his child's unwanted, arranged marriage. By following these conventions, Haywood can better utilize the "virtue in distress" paradigm, but she also expands on the romance-based conventions. For Haywood's moral purpose—to prove "how dangerous it is to give way to Passion"—she must illustrate more than that men are evil exploiters of innocent women: she must show that men do not share women's virtuous sentiments about love. Whereas women are "O'erwhelm'd in Tenderness, and lost to every Thought but that of giving Pleasure" to their lover, men often

11

possess "only that part of Desire which tends to Enjoyment . . . brutal Appetite alone." Again and again, male difference is reiterated to show the baseness of men:

> [H]e was grown weary of counterfeiting a Passion which he was incapable of feeling for her, and long'd for that Ceremony . . . which would ease him of the task of Dissimulation, and at the same time make him Master of her Fortune[.]

> Marriage, [writes one man] . . . obliges the Pair . . . to wear a *Show* of Love; but where is the Man who has one Month become a Husband, that can with truth aver he feels the same unbated Fondness for his Wife, as when her untasted Charms first won him to her Arms[.]

> *Bellcour*, altho' a Man (strange Paradox!) was less successful in Dissimulation; but he had not yet learn'd the Practices of his betraying Sex, and was not half perfect in the undoing Art.

Even Annilia's hero cannot be trusted by the reader as he admits that to find she is rich endears her to him more. The female reader of these tales discovers more and more that she can rely only on herself and her suspicions to protect her in this masculine society.

One of the innovations Haywood introduces in her male characters is an element of psychological dimension. Bellcour's tortured conscience and inner conflict between duty to his father and love for Alathia add an emotional tension to *The Double Marriage* that is lacking in the depiction of men in the other two novellas. In *The Double Marriage*, Haywood suggests that it is not so much every man's will to be false as it is his fate. In phrases reminiscent of the supernatural element in Defoe's fiction, Haywood points to the example of Bellcour—literally "beautiful heart"—and his inability to remain faithful to his secret wife: "he began to look on this Adventure, which drew him as it were whether he would or not, back to his Obedience, as if design'd by

Heaven to prevent his forsaking [his] Father. . . ." Circumstances and meetings he had wished to avoid "seem'd to him so strange a mystery of Fate" as to be predestined despite his free will.

Bellcour is a feminized male character: he is made a victim by his monetary and emotional dependence upon a more powerful man, his moral and social obligations to a superior, and his own passion. Even men are sometimes the pawns of the forces of Love, says Haywood. But Bellcour's predicament is construed as masculinely tragic rather than femininely pathetic as is Alathia's or Annilia's situation. Fate punishes Bellcour for his tragic flaw of not being able to stand up for his love against his father's ego. The reader must ask herself whether a woman, too, must not make a stand for what she wants. Alathia tries, but she needs Bellcour's support. Annilia succeeds because she has Marathon's support. Haywood stresses that harmonious partnerships between the sexes cannot exist as long as men's betraying behaviour is condoned and encouraged by a patriarchal society. As in Bellcour's case and Horatio's, fathers teach sons how to exploit women.

Haywood's novellas, which tell their stories in under sixty-five pages each and follow the particular formula of the "persecuted innocence" myth, are not without style and structure. Although she employs stereotypical characters who, therefore, cannot develop verisimilitude and depth, Haywood manages to add an interesting effect through her pairing of characters in her tales. Just as she presents the pairs of fathers and sons—Giraldo and Horatio, Maraphill and Bellcour—in *The Distress'd Orphan* and *The Double Marriage* to illustrate the perpetuation of female exploitation and the corrupt patriarchy, so Haywood also offers complementary sets of women characters to manifest different feminine responses to the restrictions of the masculine world.

In *The City Jilt*, the aggressive, vengeful Glicera is counterbalanced by her friend, Laphelia who, while helping Glicera in her plot, also tries to temper her hatred. Laphelia, who marries at the end of the story despite being witness to the falseness of men, is offered as a forgiving woman, intelligent but possessing the softer passions. Glicera, having learned dissimulation from men, essentially becomes masculine. At her story's conclusion, she lives alone, choosing to ignore men rather than attempt to compete in the world with them. The man-hater who banishes herself from society and the happily married, socially assimilated young woman demonstrate that between these two fictionalized choices for women is still a spectrum of less extreme, and therefore more realistic, female lives. Glicera' and Laphelia's endings seem to cancel each other out, suggesting that it is just as unlikely that women will avenge themselves on "that ungrateful Sex" as that they will experience the pleasures of marriage.

The Double Marriage offers Alathia and Mirtamene, both of whom take second place in the action to Bellcour's psychological drama, as characters in analogous situations. Alathia is clandestinely wed to Bellcour when he convinces her that it is the only way to delude their cruel parents; however, once Bellcour meets Mirtamene, he forgets his first wife. Alathia is abandoned and ruined, lacking proof to verify the legality of her marriage. Mirtamene is threatened by the rapist, Clavio, who tries arguments very similar to those used by Bellcour on Alathia: "the Possession of your Charms is a Blessing so necessary to my Peace, that I wou'd prefer Death . . . to a long Life without you. — Yield therefore . . . with willingness to the Joys of Love, which I swear . . . shall be inviolably kept secret." But whereas Alathia succumbs to Bellcour's "Arguments to persuade her to yield to his Desires," Mirtamene fights against Clavio's assault. However, both female characters are ultimately undone by Bellcour, with Alathia killing herself and Mirtamene forsaking men altogether.

Finally, it is in *The Distress'd Orphan* that we discover the most interesting pairing of characters, for in this work the heroine is doubled in a male character. This is not the same as Alathia's disguising herself as a man so that she may take the initiative and find out the truth about her husband's second marriage; rather, the masculinely aggressive mistress is silenced in the text and supplanted by a lesser, male character. Annilia is placed in the mad-house and replaced in her relationship with her lover by the manservant, Osephas. Osephas is made distinctively feminine through the text's language and is described in wife-like terms that emphasize his subservience, allegiance and gratitude to the hero, Marathon. In relation to his servant, Marathon is permitted to play the dominant, masculine role, reasserting his social significance which may have been in question in the love relationship with the strong Annilia. Haywood emphasizes reciprocity and interdependence in this new relationship, though. Marathon's reliance upon and willingness to learn from his socially inferior servant help him to accept this kind of mutual relationship with Annilia. Thus, Haywood attempts to work out an egalitarian relationship between the sexes. Rather than using heterosexual desire to dominate others, Haywood suggests the significance of what Hélène Cixous calls "the other bisexuality"[12] — a coming to terms with, and an appreciation of the feminine and masculine qualities in women and men.

Eliza Haywood is not simply a woman's writer, for she writes for both sexes, attempting to teach them the mutual value of social and sexual balance. James Sterling praised her as "the Proxy of vindictive Heav'n" but she was more concerned with earthly, or perhaps, earthy matters between men and women. She stated repeatedly in her dedications that her so-called pornographic works were written with a moral intention: she aimed to illustrate to women the detrimental effects of passion on their lives as it allowed men to control them more fully, while she also wished to show men that by treating women as objects of desire or measures of manhood, they were, in fact, cheating themselves of a richer, more complete life. For Haywood and her readers, sex was a dangerous, yet fascinating weapon in the battle of the sexes. The amatory novellas of Eliza Haywood depict the erotic possibilities and the social realities for both sexes as they instruct, delight and attempt to reform the age.

---

[12]Cixous, "The Laugh of the Medusa," David H. Richter, ed., *The Critical Tradition: Classic Texts and Contemporary Trends* (New York, 1989), 1096.

A NOTE ON THE TEXT

Copies of the British Library's third edition of *The Distress'd Orphan* (catalogued as BM 12611.f.14), the second edition of *The City Jilt* (catalogued as BM 012611.e.13) and the Thomas Fisher Rare Books Library's third edition of *The Double Marriage* (catalogued as B-11 B65), all dated 1726, have been used to prepare this edition. The long 's' has been eliminated throughout and running quotation marks have been omitted. Otherwise, the text has not been modernized and retains the original spelling, punctuation, capitalization and italicization to preserve the nature and spirit of Haywood's style. I have inserted a period in square brackets on page 78. On page 123, in square brackets, I have restored the sense of one line by reversing the placement of two words so that the sentence now reads ". . . the Power your Folly has given [her] over [you]" rather than the obviously incorrect in context ". . .you over her."

A CHRONOLOGY OF
ELIZA HAYWOOD

c.1693   born in London, Eliza Fowler

c.1711   marriage to the Rev. Valentine Haywood
a son, Charles, born

1715   appearance on stage in Smock Alley, Dublin, as
Chloe, in Thomas Shadwell's *Timon of Athens*

1719   *Love in Excess*, Parts 1 and 2

1720   *Love in Excess*, Part 3
The Life of Duncan Campbell (with Daniel Defoe)
Letters from a Lady of Quality to a Chevalier (French
trans.)

1721   Valentine Haywood's advertisement in *The Post
Boy* announcing wife's elopement
The Fair Captive (tragedy)
unaddressed letter seeking a patron, stating that
she has two children now

1722   *The British Recluse*
The Injur'd Husband (dated 1723)

1723   *Idalia; or, The Unfortunate Mistress*
A Wife to be Lett (comedy)
Lasselia
The Rash Resolve (dated 1724)

1724   *Poems on Several Occasions*
A Spy upon the Conjurer
The Masqueraders, Part 1
The Fatal Secret
The Surprise
The Arragonian Queen
La Belle Assemblée, Parts 1, 2 and 3 (French
trans.)
Memoirs of a Certain Island, Vol. 1 (dated 1725)
Bath Intrigues

Fantomina
The Force of Nature
Memoirs of the Baron de Brosse (dated 1725)

1725   *The Masqueraders*, Part 2
The Lady Philosopher's Stone (Fr. trans.)
The Unequal Conflict
The Tea-Table, Part 1
The Dumb Projector
Fatal Fondness
Mary Stuart
Memoirs of a Certain Island, Vol. 2 (dated 1726)

1726   *The Distress'd Orphan*
The Mercenary Lover
The Tea-Table, Part 2
Reflections on the Various Effects of Love
The City Jilt
The Double Marriage
The Court of Caramania (dated 1727)
Letters from the Palace of Fame (dated 1727)
Cleomelia (dated 1727)

1727   *The Fruitless Enquiry*
The Life of Madam de Villesache
Love in its Variety (Spanish trans.)
Philidore and Placentia
The Perplex'd Dutchess (dated 1728)

1728   *The Padlock*
The Agreeable Caledonian, Part 1
Irish Artifice (in *The Female Dunciad*)
The Disguis'd Prince, Part 1 (French. trans.)
Persecuted Virtue

1729   *The Agreeable Caledonian*, Part 2
The Fair Hebrew
Frederick, Duke of Brunswick-Lunenburgh (tragedy)
The Disguis'd Prince, Part 2 (French trans.)
satirized in Pope's *Dunciad Variorum*

1730   *Love-Letters on all Occasions*
        satirized as Mrs. Novel in Fielding's *The Author's
        Farce and The Pleasures of the Town*
        stage-appearance as Achilles' ex-mistress, Briseis,
        in William Hatchett's *Rival Father*
        stage-appearance as Mrs. Arden in *Arden of
        Feversham* which she may have adapted

1732   *Secret Memoirs of the Late Mr. Duncan Campbell*

1733   *The Opera of Operas* (musical adaptation of Field-
        ing's *Tragedy of Tragedies*, 1731)

1734   *L'Entretien des Beaux Esprits* (French trans.)

1736   *Adventures of Eovaai*

1737   stage-appearance at the New Theatre in the
        Haymarket as Mrs. Screen in Fielding's *His-
        torical Register for the Year 1736*
        stage-appearance at the Theatre Royal in Drury
        Lane as the Muse in Fielding's *Eurydice Hiss'd;
        or, A Word to the Wise*

1740   *The Unfortunate Princess* (dated 1741)

1741   Established at the Sign of Fame in Covent Gar-
        den and publication of *Anti-Pamela*
        The Busy Body (French trans.)

1742   *The Virtuous Villager* (French trans.)

1743   *A Present for a Servant-Maid*

1744   *The Fortunate Foundlings*

1744–46 *The Female Spectator* (published monthly) 4 vols.

1746   *The Parrot* (published weekly)

1748   *Life's Progress through the Passions*

1749   *Dalinda*
        Epistles for the Ladies, 2 vols. (dated 1749–50)

1750   *A Letter from H＿＿＿ G＿＿g, Esq.*
           The History of Cornelia

1751   *The History of Miss Betsy Thoughtless*, 4 vols.

1752   *The History of Jemmy and Jenny Jessamy*, 3 vols.
           (dated 1753)

1753   *Modern Characters*

1754   *The Invisible Spy*, 4 vols. (dated 1755)

1755   *The Wife* (dated 1756)

1756   *The Husband*
           The Young Lady (published 3 numbers)

           death of Eliza Haywood, February 25, 1756

POSTHUMOUS PUBLICATIONS

1768   *Clementina*
1772   *A New Present for a Servant Maid* (dated 1771)
1778   *The History of Leonora Meadowson*, 2 vols.

SELECT BIBLIOGRAPHY
OF CRITICAL STUDIES

Books

Ballaster, Ros. *Seductive Forms: Women's Amatory Fiction from 1684 to 1740*. Oxford: Clarendon Press, 1992.

Richetti, John J. *Popular Fiction before Richardson: Narrative Patterns 1700–1739*. Oxford: Oxford University Press, 1969.

Schofield, Mary Anne. *Quiet Rebellion: The Fictional Heroines of Eliza Fowler Haywood*. Washington D.C.: University Press of America, 1982.

————. *Eliza Haywood*. Boston: Twayne Publishers, 1985.

Spencer, Jane. *The Rise of the Woman Novelist: From Aphra Behn to Jane Austen*. Oxford: Blackwell, 1986.

Todd, Janet. *The Sign of Angellica: Women, Writing and Fiction 1660–1800*. New York: Columbia University Press, 1989.

Whicher, George Frisbie. *The Life and Romances of Mrs. Eliza Haywood*. New York: Columbia University Press, 1915.

Articles

Ballaster, Rosalind. "Eliza Haywood," *British Women Writers: A Critical Reference Guide*. ed. Janet Todd. London: Routledge, 1989. 322–326.

Blouch, Christine. "Eliza Haywood and the Romance of Obscurity," *Studies in English Literature* 31 (1991): 535–551.

Firmager, Gabrielle. "Eliza Haywood: Some Further Light on Her Background?" *Notes and Queries* 38 (1991): 181–183.

Kern, Jean B. "The Fallen Woman, from the Perspective of Five Early Eighteenth-Century Women Novelists," *Studies in Eighteenth-Century Culture* 10 (1981): 457–468.

London, April. "Placing the Female: The Metonymic Garden in Amatory and Pious Narrative, 1700–1740," *Fetter'd or Free? British Women Novelists, 1670–1815*. eds. Mary Anne Schofield and Cecilia Macheski. Athens: Ohio University Press, 1986. 101–123.

Richetti, John J. "Voice and Gender in Eighteenth-Century Fiction: Haywood to Burney," *Studies in the Novel* 19 (1987): 263–272.

Schofield, Mary Anne. "The Awakening of the Eighteenth-Century Heroine: Eliza Haywood's New Women," *Critic* 43 (1981): 9–13.

————. "Exposé of the Popular Heroine: The Female Protagonists of Eliza Haywood," *Studies in Eighteenth-Century Culture* 12 (1983): 93-103.

_____. " 'Descending Angels': Salubrious Sluts and Pretty Prostitutes," *Fetter'd or Free? British Women Novelists, 1670-1815.* eds. Schofield and Macheski. Athens: Ohio University Press, 1986. 186-200.

Spencer, Jane. "Eliza Haywood," *A Dictionary of British and American Women Writers 1660-1800*, ed. Janet Todd. Totowa, New Jersey: Rowman & Littlefield, 1987. 157-160.

Wilputte, Earla A. "Gender Inversions in Haywood's *The Distress'd Orphan, or, Love in a Mad-house,*" *Lumen XIV (forthcoming).*

ABBREVIATIONS

Ashton   John Ashton, *Social Life in the Reign of Queen*
                  Anne, 2 vols. (London, 1882).
Blackstone   Sir William Blackstone, *Commentaries on the*
                  Laws of England, 4 vols. (Oxford, 1765).
Cunnington   C. Willett and Phillis Cunnington, *Handbook*
                  of English Costume in the Eighteenth Century
                  (London, 1957).
Grosart   *The Complete Works in Prose of Abraham Cowley*,
                  2 vols., ed. Alexander B. Grosart (New
                  York, 1967).
OED   *Oxford English Dictionary*
Stone   Lawrence Stone, *Uncertain Unions: Marriage in*
                  England 1660–1753 (Oxford, 1992).
Tilley   M.P. Tilley, *A Dictionary of the Proverbs in*
                  England in the Sixteenth and Seventeenth Centuries
                  (Ann Arbor, 1966).
Webster's   *The New Lexicon Webster's Encyclopedic Dictionary*
                  of the English Language, Canadian ed. (New
                  York, 1972).
Wolfram   Sybil Wolfram, *In-Laws and Outlaws: Kinship*
                  and Marriage in England (London, 1987).

THE

DISTRESS'D ORPHAN,

OR

L O V E

IN A

M A D-H O U S E.

—————*No Lover has the power*

To enforce a desperate Amour,

Like him that has two Strings to's Bow,

And burns for Love and Money too:

For then he's brave and resolute,

Disdains to render in his Suit;

Has all his Flames and Raptures double,

And hangs or drowns with half the Trouble.

HUDIBRAS.[1]

---

[1]The epigraph is taken from Samuel Butler's burlesque mock-epic poem, *Hudibras* (1663–1678), Part 3, canto 1, lines 1–8.

Love in a Mad-House

ANNILIA was the Daughter of an eminent Merchant of a City, which boasts more wealthy Men of that Profession than perhaps any other part of the World: She had the misfortune to lose both her Parents before she arrived at an Age capable of knowing what it was to be an Orphan; and, indeed, the Care and Tenderness with which she was treated by her Guardian, who was also her Uncle, left her for a time no possibility of regretting her Condition; perceiving she had a Genius rare to be found in a Person of her Sex, he had the best Masters to instruct her in the *French*, *Latin*, and *Italian* Tongues, as also in the more ordinary Accomplishments of her Sex, such as Musick, Dancing, Singing, and many fine Works; in all which she grew so early a Proficient, that People scarce knew which most to admire, her extraordinary Capacity, or the uncommon Care and Indulgence with which her Uncle studied to improve it. But alas! a little time discover'd that *Giraldo*, for so he was call'd, had other Views than those he at present made a show of, and that it was not meerly for her own sake, that he endeavour'd to imbellish her Mind.

He had a Son named *Horatio*, about six Years elder than *Annilia*; they were bred together, and from their most tender Ages he endeavour'd to inspire in the Breast of both a mutual Tenderness for each other; whether in the Study or the Dancing-School, they scarce were ever asunder; the same Tutors and Masters instructed both, and in all the Improvements or Diversions of their Youth, they still went equal Sharers. This manner of proceeding could not but create a very great Fondness between them; which he observing, doubted not but when they came to Years capable of entertaining other Desires, they would be possess'd of such as the great Fortune *Annilia* was to be Mistress of, made him wish to

27

inspire in them. He communicated not his Designs to any one till she was arrived at the Age of fourteen,[2] about which time *Horatio* was twenty, and then thinking it a fitting Season, resolved no longer to delay the Accomplishment of them. His Son was the first Person whose Inclinations he thought proper to sound, and taking him one day into his Closet, *Horatio, said he*, I have observed of late a Kindness between you and your fair Cousin, which makes me think there is something in your Hearts more tender for each other, than what the Ties of Blood occasions; if it be so, I would not have you make a Secret of it, I know no body more deserving the warmest Affection than *Annilia*, and you need not doubt my Consent to your mutual Happiness. Nothing could be more surprized than was *Horatio* at this Demand; beautiful and witty as this young Charmer was, he had never been sensible of any other Inclinations for her, than such as a Brother might avow for a Sister; nor had so much as once thought of her in the manner his Father seem'd to intimate. The little Hesitation which he made in answering, confirm'd his Father in the Truth of what he said, and he found that the Measures he had taken had not been altogether so effectual as he could have wished, or had hoped: Well, but, *resumed he*, suppose 'tis my Desire to see you the Husband of *Annilia*, you would not sure incur my Displeasure, by refusing me that Proof of your Obedience. *Horatio*, who, tho' far from feeling the Emotions of a Lover, had a just Regard and Friendship for her, presently reply'd, that he should not be refractory to his Commands, tho' it were to something more difficult than this; declaring at the same time, that tho' he had no Inclinations for entring into that State he mention'd, yet since it was his pleasure he should do so, he would comply without Reluctance.

[2]*Age of fourteen* A girl orphan "at fourteen is at years of legal discretion, and may choose a guardian." Giraldo, Annilia's guardian, is eager to initiate a marriage so early with his son before the girl may decide to find another guardian. At twelve years of age, a girl orphan was "at years of maturity, and therefore [could] consent or diasgree to marriage, and, if proved to have sufficient discretion, [could] bequeath her personal estate" (Blackstone, Bk. I, chap. 17, 451). Giraldo wishes, therefore, to secure Annilia's estate for his own family as soon as possible.

You little study your own Interest, if you do not, *said* Giraldo; the Estate which *Annilia* is possessed of, join'd to your own, will make you the greatest Man that ever has been of our Family. 'Tis therefore my Desire, that if you cannot in reality entertain a Passion for her, you will at least feign to have done so; and while you are disposing yourself for that purpose, I will prepare her for the Declaration you are to make. *Horatio* having once more assured him of his Obedience, went out of the Room, and *Annilia* being that moment passing by, was call'd in by *Giraldo*, and after reminding her of the Obligations she had to him for the Care he had taken of her Education, and the fatherly Tenderness of his Behaviour to her, My dear Niece! *said he*, I speak not these things to you, as doubting your grateful Acknowledgment, but because that the Remembrance of my Kindness may make you know, that 'tis impossible for to advise you to any thing, which I am not confident is for your Good. — You are now of an Age which will expose you to Temptations greater than at present you can have any Notion of — my House will soon be crowded with a great number of those, whom either the Charms of your Person or Estate will induce to call themselves your Lovers. — Young as you are, you cannot but have observed how many have been deceived by a fictitious Pretence of that Passion — a Woman therefore cannot too early put herself out of the way of these Deluders by Marriage, provided she has an Offer which those who have the Care of her, find to her advantage. — What say you, *Annilia*, *pursued he*, have you ever yet had any serious Thoughts of a Husband? The innocent Maid blushed extremely at an Interrogatory she so little expected; but having a little recover'd herself from her Confusion, Pardon me, Sir! *said she*, if I think a Question of this kind pretty odd to a Person of my Years,[3] who has never borrowed so much time from those Studies you have been so good to prescribe to me, as to think on things so far remote as

---

[3]*a Question of this kind. . .of my Years* In the seventeenth and eighteenth centuries, marriage was usually delayed to a decade after puberty, "that is to about 26 to 28 for men and 24 to 26 for women" (Stone, 10). Naturally, Annilia, at fourteen years of age, would find Giraldo's question "pretty odd."

Love and Marriage, and which perhaps 'twill never be my Lot to experience. That were to disappoint the End for which you were created, *reply'd* Giraldo; nor will you long retain Sentiments like these: to prevent therefore an Alteration in them in favour of some Man unworthy of you, I would have you endeavour to settle your Affections on one, who you are certain will always love you, and who is your Equal in every thing but Wealth. Still as he spoke, the Confusion of *Annilia* increas'd, she blushed, she trembled, Shame and Fear by turns assailed her, yet was she not presently able to account for either; but not being perfectly assured whether her Uncle spoke in this manner to try her Temper, or if he were really in earnest, As I cannot comprehend what 'tis you mean, Sir, *said she*, I am at a loss to give a direct Reply; but of this am very certain, that to whatever you think for my good, I shall submit with readiness, having learnt thus much from my Studies, that I shall never be able to know so well what is best for me, as those do, from whom I received that Knowledge which I have. This Modesty becomes you, *return'd he*, would all young Women yield to the Reasons of their Friends[4] with like Humility, how few of your Sex would mourn the sad Effects of ill-placed Love! But why, *Annilia, continued he*, do you think yourself too young to marry, you see nothing is more common than for Persons of your Age to enter into that State? Is it because you are willing to wait till some violent Passion instigates you to it? Or have you an Aversion to the Name of Wife? Neither, Sir, *answer'd she*, I faithfully assure you: As for the first, I look on myself to be of a Humour, which will never suffer me to fall into those Extravagancies I have been witness of in some of my Acquaintance; and as for the other, I am so far from having any dislike to a Married-State, that I believe it the most happy of any, provided there be no disparity either in the Minds or Fortunes of the Pair so united. What think you then, *said he*, of *Horatio?* I know of no great Inequality between my Son and you—Your Tempers have hitherto been perfectly agreeable to each other—He is, indeed, at present less possess'd of the Goods of Fortune; but in time, per-

[4]*Friends* relatives, kinsfolk, people (OED).

haps, he may not be unworthy of you even in that respect. My Cousin! *cry'd she, strangely amazed.* Yes, *pursued* Giraldo, he has this moment revealed to me the Passion he has for you, tho' the Respect which always accompanies true Love, has hitherto kept him from declaring it to yourself.—What say you, my dear Niece! *added he,* must he despair? Will not all the Friendship you have received from his Father, join'd to his own Merits and unbounded Affection, be sufficient to compensate for what he wants in Riches. O think me not, *answer'd she,* of so mean and sordid a Soul, as to prefer Wealth and Grandeur to those Virtues *Horatio* is possess'd of.—My Cousin has certainly all the good Qualities a Woman would wish to find in him she chuses for a Companion for Life: and if I did not immediately guess him to be the Person, when you described the Man to whom you wished to see me join'd in Wedlock, it was only because of the Affinity between us—Methinks we are too near already by Blood, to be made more near by Marriage. Not in the least, *said* Giraldo, there is no Law either divine or human, which forbids the Nuptials of Brothers Children[5]—I could instance many Examples of the greatest and the best, to prove it is allowed by all Religions; but I hope, *continued he,* they are needless: the Precepts which I have always endeavour'd to instill in your Mind, are such as will give you no ground to think I would persuade you to an Act either unwarrantable or disadvantageous. I have done with my Objections, Sir! *reply'd* Annilia; but give me leave to think on what you have said, and in obedience to your Desires, will endeavour to convert that sisterly Affection, which at present warms my Heart, to something more soft and passionate in fa-

---

[5]*the Nuptials of Brothers Children* ". . . in 1603 the Church of England adopted a Table of Levitical Degrees [entitled 'A Table of Kindred & Affinity, wherein whosoever are related are forbidden in scripture and our laws to marry together') proposed by Archbishop Parker in 1563. . . .Archbishop Parker's Table forbade marriage between all relations in and within the third degree of consanguinity and affinity"; that is, one could not marry one's mother/father, aunt/uncle, grandparent, sibling, child, niece/nephew, grandchild (including one's stepbrother/sister, step-child, step-grandchild nor any of the above "in-laws") (Wolfram, 26). In other words, Annilia could legally marry her cousin Horatio.

vour of *Horatio*. She had no sooner spoke these Words, than she went out of the Closet, leaving *Giraldo* perfectly satisfy'd with the Conversation which had passed between them.

After this, the Father and Son redoubled the Civilities with which they had been accustom'd to treat her; and the latter of them omitted nothing of those Arts which Men make use of, when they would be thought passionately in love: She listen'd neither with pleasure nor disquiet to the Declarations he made her, and 'tis not to be doubted but that she would in a little time have yielded to become his Wife, had not that Passion, to which she hitherto had been a Stranger, on a sudden interposed, and made her sensible that there were Joys in Marriage, which the faint Esteem she could bring herself to feel for *Horatio*, would never let her experience with him.

An Entertainment being given at the House of a neighbouring Lady, *Horatio* and *Annilia* were among the number of the Invited, as was also a fine young Gentleman lately arrived from a foreign Country, where he had pass'd some time in the Exercise of Arms; tho' bred to War, he was not ignorant of the Accomplishments which grace a Court, and to the most agreeable Person in the World, he had also added all the Perfections which make Conversation pleasing. *Annilia* look'd on him as something divine, and from the moment of his first entring the Room, felt Agitations such as she never before had been acquainted with; nor did he view her with less Amaze, not all his Travels had presented him with an Object so engageing; never did the God of Love send swifter or more piercing Darts, than those he now fixed in the Hearts of this equally charming, equally charmed Pair — Both as yet were too much Strangers to the Passion they had so lately entertain'd, to know the Reason of so strange an Alteration in themselves, much less had they the power of making use of any Artifice to conceal it from the Observation of others: But Colonel *Marathon*, for by that Name shall I distinguish this young Hero, whether it were to his being some Years older than *Annilia*, or that his Emotions were more violent than hers, that he owed being the first Discoverer of their mutual Passion, is uncertain; but long it was not before he not only knew he was a Lover, but also that the

beautiful Object of his Affections looked not on him with the
Eyes of Indifference: and this Encouragement, join'd to the becoming Boldness of his Profession, took from him those little
Fears, which generally accompany the first Thrillings of Inclination, and compel the over-awed Adorer to restrain his Languishments, and carefully conceal from the dear Inspirer, what perhaps she longs with equal Ardency to be told. Having therefore
been inform'd by some of the Company, of whom he had enquir'd, that she was not married, he resolved to make use of the
first Opportunity which should present itself, to let her know
before they parted, the Effect her Charms had work'd upon his
Soul. But this was not so easy a Matter to be accomplish'd as he
had imagin'd, *Horatio* had taken notice of the distant Regards he
paid her, and for that reason kept close to her, to prevent him
from engaging her in any private Conversation; nor could he
entertain her with any thing but in general Terms, and what
might pass for his Complaisance to the other Ladies as well as to
her; till the Collation being over, some of the Company proposed
Country Dancing, which being comply'd with, tho' *Horatio* had
Annilia for his Partner, the assiduous Lover found the means to
let her know he was so, saying a thousand tender things whenever he pass'd by her, turn'd her by the Hand, or the Figure of the
Dance gave him an Opportunity of leading her aside; but thinking these too ineffectual Demonstrations of his Passion, he made
an Excuse to step into another Room, he desir'd Pen and Paper,
and writ a Declaration of his Mind in these Terms.

To the most *Adorable* ANNILIA.

THO' I doubt not but my Eyes have given all who have observed their Glances, sufficient Intelligence of my Heart; yet
lest you should be ignorant of their Language, vouchsafe to
learn it from my Pen — 'Tis too much to suffer the Wound, yet
be deny'd the Privilege of complaining — I love you, O Divinest
of your Sex! I need not tell you with a Flame as honourable as it
is sincere and ardent; for sure so heavenly an Innocence as
shines about you, can inspire no other Wishes but such as bear
some Conformity to itself — Nor can my Zeal be supposed to

arise from any mercenary View, as yet I know no more of you than your Name, and not yet disposed of in Marriage, for which last Information I bless indulgent Fate — Your Birth and Fortune are things indifferent, provided I may not hear they are above my Hopes; yet might I have my Wish, 'twould be, that you had no other Dowry than the Treasure of your Charms, that I might prove 'twas you, and only you, I would possess — But be you whatever Heaven is pleased to make you, you are and must be the Sovereign Mistress of my Soul, and the only Disposer of my future Destiny. I see well I have a Rival in presence, which has made me take this way of declaring, what it is impossible to conceal and live — I shall make it my business to inform myself what Place you make happy by dwelling in it, and throw myself at your Feet for a Pardon for this Presumption; in the mean time, conjure you to think with Pity on

Your Eternally Devoted Slave,
MARATHON.

Having made up this Billet,[6] he return'd to the Company, where he had not been many Minutes, before a Gentleman happening to take notice of a fine Piece of Painting at the lower end of the Room, every body was crowding near to observe the Beauties of it; among the rest, the Curiosity of *Annilia* was excited, and as she was following *Horatio* some Steps behind him, Madam, *said the watchful Lover, putting into her Hand the Letter*, I found this directed for you, and imagin'd it might fall from your Pocket by some Accident. These Words, and the Sight of the Superscription, made all the Face of *Annilia* of the same Colour with her Cheeks; and fearing to do any thing which might give an imprudent Encouragement, It cannot be mine, Sir! *reply'd she*, I receive no Letters directed in this manner. With these Words she would have returned it to him,

---

[6]*Billet* usually referred to as *billet-doux*; love-letter (from the French, "sweet note") (OED). Haywood may be punning by using this short form as soldiers (like Colonel Marathon) were often billeted, that is, assigned quarters or lodging.

but putting back her Hand, It has your Name upon it, Madam, *said he*, and 'tis probable the Contents may not be so proper to be read by any other — 'tis convenient therefore you take care of it. As he spoke these Words, he turn'd away, and mingled with those who were admiring the Picture, leaving *Annilia* so cover'd with Shame and Confusion, that instead of prosecuting her Design of joining with the others in praising the Painter's Art, she threw herself into a Chair, and was ready to faint at the Apprehensions of what the Consequences might be of this Day's Adventure — She trembled at the encroaching Passion of her own Soul — was alarmed at the Boldness of her Lover — dreaded the Jealousy of *Horatio*, and almost died, to find that nothing now was so terrible as the Thoughts of being his Wife — In this Condition did the Company, as they were returning to their Seats, find her; and all the Tokens of a violent Disorder being on her, *Horatio* asked her if she would not go home; to which Demand she answering in the Affirmative, they took leave, and went into the Chariot of *Giraldo*, which was waiting at the Door.

The Suddenness of her Indisposition and Departure, made the Conversation for some time after she was gone, turn on no other Subject; which gave the Colonel an Opportunity of hearing where she lived, her Fortune, and the Circumstances she was in with her Guardian, who having of late made no Secret of marrying her to his Son, was highly blamed by some People, as consulting more his own Interest, than the Advantage of the young Lady committed to his Care, whose Person and Estate, they all agreed, might entitle her to a much greater Expectation.

Colonel *Marathon* found in this Account enough both to torment and please him, tho' he was really of a generous Disposition, and had a Stock of Love for *Annilia*, which would have compensated for all the Deficiencies of Wealth or Grandeur; yet there are Charms in Riches, which still more endear a lovely Person, and in spite of what he had said in his Letter, he could not find in his heart to think it a Misfortune, that the Woman he was in love with had those Recommendations; but the knowledge that the Person who had so much the power over her Actions, had destined her to another, and the Difficulties which he foresaw he had to struggle with in the Pursuit of his Affections, gave him Disquiets which it would be impossible to represent.

The Consideration of the Obstacles he should meet with, was not however of any force to deter him from proceeding; he resolv'd, that if he must despair, it should not be occasion'd by his own Negligence, or Remissness. And not believing that *Horatio* had taken notice of his Behaviour, he went the next day to the House of *Giraldo*, and boldly enquiring for *Horatio*, the Servants, who judging by his Appearance that he was a Man of Fashion, desired him to walk into the Parlour, where the whole Family were at that time sitting together. *Horatio*, who had acquainted his Father that a strange Gentleman had paid a more that ordinary Devoir[7] to his Cousin, look'd first on him, and then on the Colonel, with a kind of Consternation. *Giraldo*, who knew not the meaning of his Son's Surprize, nor that this was the Person he suspected for his Rival, knew not what to think, till the Colonel eased him of his Suspence, by speaking in this manner: Nothing but the Occasion, Sir, *said he*, could excuse the seeming Rudeness of this Visit: I confess I was as sincerely grieved at this Lady's Indisposition last Night (*pursued he, bowing to* Annilia, *with a Tenderness which the Presence of his Rival did not oblige him to conceal*) as I am rejoiced to find her thus perfectly recover'd; and it was as much to enquire after her Health, as to improve my little Acquaintance with your Son, that I took the liberty of waiting on you. Neither *Giraldo* nor *Horatio* could avoid using him with good Breeding, but the manner of their Civilities appeared so forced, that it was easy for him to perceive that it was to that alone he was indebted, and that he was far from being a welcome Guest. — *Annilia* spoke little, and what she said was accompany'd with Blushes and Hesitation, which were no way pleasing to her Uncle or intended Husband, both of them with reason believ-

----

[7]*Devoir* dutiful respect, courteous attention (OED).

ing, that such Disorders could not be occasion'd but by some unusual Agitation of the Spirits. The Colonel perceived it also, and with a Satisfaction equal to the Chagrin of the others; but finding there was no probability of speaking to *Annilia*, but in the Presence of those two Gentlemen, he staid but a short time, concluding his Visit with a Desire they would return, and under the pretence of letting them know where they might do so, acquainted them with the Place of his Abode: but the real Design of his telling them, was with the hope that the fair Object of his Affections might have entertain'd a Passion for him violent enough to engage her to answer his Letter. But he knew little of her Soul, to flatter himself with such a Thought; she loved him, indeed, but Modesty, and that Decorum which all Women, who know the Value of themselves, ought to observe, would not suffer her to do any thing for the Gratification of her softer Wishes, which should render her cheap in the Opinion of the Man, whose Esteem she desired to attract.

The Colonel had no sooner left them, than her Ears were persecuted with the incessant Railings of the Father and the Son; one exclaim'd against his Shape and Air, the other found a thousand Faults with his Conversation and Manner of Address; but most of all they seem'd to blame his Assurance, in visiting Persons to whom he was so much a Stranger. It was with the utmost difficulty that she restrain'd herself from vindicating him, but Love had now taught her the Art of disguising her Sentiments, to which before she had been wholly a Stranger; to ease herself therefore of a Constraint so troublesome to her, she retired to her Chamber, and there gave a Loose to Thought and Meditation.

This second View of the engaging Colonel had fixed the Impression which the first had made; she could not with patience think of being the Wife of any other Man, the Sight of *Horatio* was now grown Poison to her Eyes, and nothing troubled her so much, as that she had given him hope of being his; she had made a kind of half Promise to her Uncle, which she now knew not how to retract, without letting him into the Reason of that Change in her Humour; and to do that, not only the innate Modesty of her Temper, but her Passion also forbid, as making her not doubt, but that if he should once come to know she loved any other Man, much more *Marathon*, of whom he express'd so great a Dislike, he would omit nothing to disappoint her Hopes. She therefore thought it best to continue the same Behaviour to him as she had been accustomed to treat him with, at least till she found how far the Colonel would proceed in the Addresses he had begun to make: not that she design'd to marry the other, even if he should desist; but she imagin'd, that to throw him off on a sudden, would not only give him a Suspicion of the Cause, but also rouze all that he had of Rage in his Disposition, to some Act of Revenge.

This Resolution was certainly the most discreet one she could take, yet was it not in her power long to maintain it. The next day, as they were all at Dinner, the Footman acquainted them that a young Man, a Stranger, was at the Door, and said he brought a Letter for Madam *Annilia*, but that he would neither deliver it to any Hand but her own, nor reveal from whom he came. Her Blushes, in spite of her Efforts to restrain them, betray'd to the observing *Giraldo*, that she guess'd who 'twas that sent it; and being about to open her Mouth, either to forbid, or order the Person to be admitted, which she was herself scarce determin'd, vexed to the heart that *Marathon*, for she imagined it no other, should be so indiscreet to send in that publick manner, when her Uncle saved her the trouble, by bidding his Servant turn the Fellow from the Door, and tell him that *Annilia* received no Letters, but what were first communicated to him. She utter'd nothing in opposition to this Command, but as soon as the Servant was gone about the Execution of it, I think, Sir! *said she, with a Countenance which sufficiently denoted the highest Discontent*, the Message you have sent a pretty odd one — I am now past my Childhood, and People must imagine that I am either very deficient in Understanding, or you in the Care of improving it, when they shall be told I am incapable of judging what Answer is fit for me to give to any Letter which is sent to me. These Words, pronounced with a Spirit and Vehemence which *Giraldo* had never

before observed in her, gave him no small Surprize; but smother-
ing the secret Spite he conceived at them, You misconstrue, *said
he*, my dear Niece, this manner of proceeding; did I act otherwise, you would be continually persecuted either with begging
Petitions for the Relief of some decay'd Family, or the impudent
Addresses of some presuming Coxcomb; it was doubtless from
one of these that this Letter was sent, had it been any thing
worthy of your regard, that Caution would have been unneces-
sary, which prevented the Delivery of it before your Guardian, or
the Man intended for your Husband. The mention of that Name
threw off all the little Remains of Patience *Annilia* had preserved,
and with an Air wholly composed of Fierceness, He is not yet so,
answer'd she, and to whatever Subjection I may be destined after
Marriage,[8] I take it ill that my Liberty should be restrain'd till
then. With these Words she rose from the Table, and retired into
her Chamber, where having shut herself in, not all the Intreaties
of *Horatio*, who, to alleviate the Severity his Father had used to
her, counterfeited the most dying Lover, could prevail on her to
come forth.

Colonel *Marathon*, for it was no other who had sent that Letter, was not greatly disappointed at the Return of his Messenger; he imagin'd not it would reach her Hands, by the Wat-
chfulnes with which he perceived she was tended by *Giraldo* and
Horatio, and had only done this as a Tryal to assure himself how
far she was the Mistress of her Actions; and finding he must go
another way to work, he made it his business to discover which
of the Servants most particularly belong'd to her. He gave a
very handsome Present to one of them, accompany'd with a
Letter, which the Fellow very faithfully deliver'd to her, unseen
by any other of the Family; the Contents of it were as follows.

[8]*Subjection. . .after Marriage* "By marriage, the husband and wife are one person
in law: that is, the very being or legal existence of the woman is suspended
during the marriage, or at least is incorporated and consolidated into that of the
husband: under whose wind, protection and *cover*, she performs every thing"
(Blackstone, Bk. I, chap. 15, 430).

To the most Charming and Divine
ANNILIA.

WHAT cannot Love like mine accomplish? Surrounded as you are with more than *Argus*'s Eyes,[9] industrious Passion finds the means of reaching you. Oh could it but inspire you also with some part of that abundant store with which my Heart is full, how much beyond the faint Description of all that Words can speak, would be the Happiness of my State? — Yet think not my Wishes too presuming, with all Humility would I attend, till Time and my future Services should testify me less unworthy than at present I must appear of so exalted a Blessing; but oh I have a Rival, whose Interest more than his Merits gives me pain; were I but assured that it was more to the Obligations you may imagine yourself under to *Giraldo*, than the Tenderness you have for *Horatio*, that the latter of them has your Permission to adore you, I should then hope that the Constancy of my Flame might hereafter warm you into a just Sensibility, and Truth and Love make up the Deficiencies of all other Deserts — I now dare intreat no more, than that you will be so good to put a period to the Suspence I labour under, by informing me if Love or Grati-tude be the Motive which induces you to favour the Pretensions of *Horatio*; if to the former he is indebted for the Blessing, think more generously of my Passion than to imagine I would aim to separate Hearts united by that Tye, tho my own break in relin-quishing my Endeavours; but if to the latter it is that he owes his Hopes, permit me also to rival him in them, and believe there is no Proof of Passion you can receive from him, which will not be exceeded by

Your ever Faithful and most
passionately Devoted
MARATHON.

P.S. Since it is in the power of one Line to ease you of the Trouble of any future Sollicitations from me, and to decide my

---

[9]*Argus's Eyes* Argus was a mythological creature fabled to have had a hundred eyes. A figurative way of saying that Annilia is carefully watched by her uncle and cousin.

Fate, be so divinely generous to afford it, and either at once destroy me, by avowing your Affection for my Rival; or relieve my Anxieties, by permitting me to hope I may in time alledge an equal Plea for Favour.

Annilia thought it would be straining Modesty to a pitch too high, to refuse answering this Letter; she found nothing in either of those she had received from him but what testify'd the strictest Honour; nor did she think the World could condemn her of Indiscretion in following her Inclinations, since he was of a Family superior to her own, and possessed of a Fortune equal to that of *Horatio*, tho nothing in competition with that which she was Mistress of, might entitle her to expect with another. He was however the only Man in the World which had the power of inspiring her with that Passion which equals all things. After a very little time of Consideration therefore, she set herself to prepare an Answer for him, which was in these Lines.

To Colonel MARATHON.

MY own Reason informing me, that to hold a Correspondence of this kind, without the Privity and Approbation of the Person to whose Care I am entrusted, is among the things which are justly esteem'd blameable; I must in vindication of myself, as well as to comply with your Request, acquaint you, that the visible Self-Interestedness of my Uncle has destroy'd that Confidence I should otherwise repose in so near a Relation, and obliged me to take a Resolution never from henceforward to consult him in any Affair, in which there is a possibility of his being byass'd by a sinister View — My Circumstances, however, not permitting me to break off with him immediately, I give you no small proof of the good Opinion I have of you, when I thus freely make you Partaker of my Sentiments on this score; and after what I have said, I leave it to yourself to judge if it be to either of the Motives you mention, that *Horatio* is indebted for the Complaisance which at present he receives from me — If the Messenger who brought me yours, continues faithful to his

Trust, I permit you to write to me by the same means—I am inclined to believe you have Honour and Good-nature, and am half afraid I shall soon have occasion for a Friend possessed of these Qualifications; if such a Time arrives, I shall make tryal how far you are desirous of obliging

ANNILIA.

Having finished this little Epistle, she call'd the Servant who had been the Bearer of that to which it was a Reply; and having obliged him to swear an inviolable Secrecy, put it into his hands, assuring him of her rewarding his Fidelity, in case he persevered in it to the end; on which, he again renewing the Protestations he before had made, went joyfully to the Colonel, not doubting but he should receive from him a second Gratification for the good Success of his Negotiation: nor did his Expectations deceive him, the transported Lover was generous even beyond his hopes, and taking the surest way of binding one of his Rank to his Interest, by making it to his advantage to be honest, had the Opportunity every day of conveying to his Mistress the tender Emotions of his Soul, and receiving from her Answers which no way gave a check to the Boldness of his now-aspiring Hopes.

Nor was this distant Conversation all the Happiness he enjoy'd in his Time of Courtship. *Annilia* went very frequently to the *Opera*, Play-house, and other publick Diversions, and never miss'd her Devotions at Chappel once a day; of which *Marathon* being informed either by a Billet from herself, or by the Mouth of the same Emissary who convey'd his Letters, never failed of being present; and tho' the Presence of *Horatio*, who always accompany'd her to all these Places, prevented their Tongues from speaking the Language of their Hearts: yet what they wanted to express in Words, intelligible Looks sufficiently disclosed: she read in his Eyes unutterable Love, and all the eager Sparklings of Desire; and he had the Satisfaction to observe in hers a soft Compliance, and delightful Tenderness. But fatal to their mutual Peace was the too little Caution which both of them preserv'd; the Penetration of *Horatio* soon made him no Stranger to the Meaning of these intermixing Glances: but forbearing to alarm *Annilia* by any Marks of Jealousy or Discontent, he communicated his Sentiments to *Giraldo*, who joining in them, and the rather, because she had of late shunn'd all Conversation with them as much as was possible, and would sometimes shut herself into her Chamber half a day together, resolved some way or other to fathom the Mystery. She had never stirred abroad for a long time, but in the Company either of himself or Son; he therefore was certain that the Colonel could have no opportunity of declaring himself her Lover, unless it were by Letter; and remembring with how much warmth she had resented his refusing admittance to the Person who had one day brought one, which he made no doubt came from him, it presently came into his head, that he had found some other way of sending to her. He distrusted his Servants, and examin'd them all one by one, as well those who belonged to *Annilia*, as the rest; but all of them resolutely denying that they knew any such Person as Colonel *Marathon*, he knew not what to think — But he who was really the entrusted Person, having been sifted as well as his Fellows, acquainting the Lovers with what had passed, obliged them to be more careful for the future.

For a little time longer were they permitted the Happiness of corresponding with each other, but a Footman of *Giraldo* by accident one day seeing *Osepha*, for that was the Name of the Confidante of this Amour, come out of the House where he had heard his Master say was lodged the so much talk'd of and dreaded *Marathon*, either thro Envy of the Profit, which he doubted not his Fellow reaped by this Adventure, or to ingratiate himself, immediately ran to *Giraldo* with the News; and *Osepha*, at his Return home, was seized by both his enraged Masters, his Pockets search'd, and that Day's Letter expos'd to their Perusal; after which they had him severely beaten, his Livery pluck'd off, and turn'd out of doors. The Contents of the Billet which fell into their hands, were to this purpose.

43

To the Divine Empress of my Soul,
the most transporting ANNILIA.

EXquisitely good as you are in all things, why will you still refuse Compliance to that Advice which alone can make you easy, and which you must receive from all who are not partial to the Interest of the Mercenary *Giraldo*, and his Son, as well as from me — To prove that it is not for any Advantage of my own, I wish you to chuse another Guardian, I desire not to be the Person; only I entreat it may not be one whose Indigence or Baseness may influence him to have the same Designs on you as you have experienced from this unworthy Uncle: — depend upon it, those who have done so much to bring you to their Measures, will dare yet more; and when they once come to know, as soon they will, oblige you to declare your Sentiments. I tremble to think what horrid Use they may make of the Power you suffer them to retain over you — O prevent it, I conjure you — if no more, quit at least the House of these designing Men, or I fear you will too late repent rejecting the Fears of

Your Zealously Devoted,
MARATHON.

The Prophecy of this amorous Fool, *said* Giraldo, as soon as he had read it, may instruct us what to do; I will anon press her to comply with the speedy Celebration of the Marriage with you, or take such Measures as will compel her to it. *Horatio* was extremely pleased with this Design, he was grown weary of counterfeiting a Passion which he was incapable of feeling for her, and long'd for that Ceremony to be over, which would ease him of the task of Dissimulation, and at the same time make him Master of her Fortune. In the mean time, *Annilia*, who knew nothing of what had happen'd, was amaz'd she saw not *Osepha* with a Letter from her dear Colonel; and hastily calling for him, *Giraldo* went into her Chamber: I have just now, *said he*, discharged that Wretch you call for, but will provide you of one more honest in his Room. Discharg'd him! *cry'd she*, (strangely surpriz'd) for what Crime? The Story is too long to repeat, *resum'd he*, 'tis sufficient that I know him to be a

Villain. — Something more material engag'd my coming into your Apartment — Have you yet fix'd on the Day which is to make *Horatio* happy? You will not certainly keep longer in suspence, the Man who many Weeks ago received the Promise of being made your Husband. I know of no such Promise, *reply'd she peevishly*; I said, indeed, I would endeavour to be conformable to your Desires — and in what, *interrupted he*, is *Horatio* deficient, that those Endeavours should not be all that is requisite for his Wishes? Perhaps I yet have never ask'd myself the Question, *said she haughtily*; a Lover ought to attend with Patience the Resolution of the Woman he pretends to adore — nor will I give any direct Answer, till you resolve me for what reason you have discharg'd my Servant. You will not? *cry'd he in an angry Tone.* No, Sir! I will not, *return'd she, in one which demonstrated she was equally incensed.* This Behaviour, *resum'd he*, makes me believe you never meant but to deceive me, and had no serious Thoughts of marrying with *Horatio.* If I had, *said she*, such Arbitrary Proceedings would make me exchange them for others, which would afford at least a show of greater Satisfaction: — The Love of Liberty is natural to all, and I should have more reason to regret, than be pleas'd with the large Fortune left me by my Father, if it must subject me to eternal Slavery. You will have reason, indeed, to regret it, *answer'd he*, if by it you are expos'd to Temptations, you are too weak to resist: — In fine, *continu'd he*, I have good reason to believe your Indiscretions have of late rendred you liable to the Censure of the World, and must therefore restrain that Liberty you have but too much abused. Mild and gentle as *Annilia* was by Nature, the Injustice of this Accusation put her beyond all Patience. Good Heaven! is it possible, *cry'd she*, that you can go so far as to asperse my Conduct? — to what in time will you not have Recourse? — is this the Treatment I expected from the Brother of my Father? — But there is a way to ease myself. — There is, *reply'd he*, immediately, but no other than by speedily consenting to marry with *Horatio.* That will I never do, *said she*, perceiving that now Dissimulation was of no further Use. 'Tis well, *rejoin'd he*, you are grown strangely arrogant, but I believe I have the means to humble this unbe-

coming Pride. As he spoke these Words, he flung out of the
Room, leaving her involv'd in a mixture of Surprize, and Rage,
and Grief—so Violent were all these Passions, that for a time
she had not the Power of forming any Resolution; but when she
had, it was to quit the House of this injurious Uncle with all
imaginable speed: she order'd her Woman therefore to go out
and prepare a Lodging for her in some pleasant and agreeable
Part of the Town, while she in the mean time was busily employ'd in packing up her Clothes and Jewels.

Giraldo, who, with his Son *Horatio*, was walking in the Parlor
consulting in what manner they should now proceed with the
intended Victim of their avaritious Designs, saw her Woman
pass by them, and go hastily toward the Street-door: as she was
about to open it, he call'd her in, and having been hir'd by him,
and looking on him as her Master, she durst no other than obey,
nor had the Courage to conceal, when ask'd the Question, on
what Errand she was going. On which they look'd on each other
with a kind of an Amazement, as not having been able to
imagine she had Resolution enough to have carried her so great
a length. But *Giraldo*, whose Policy in any Affair where his own
Interest was concerned had seldom suffer'd itself to be baffled,
had a sudden Thought come into his Head which seem'd to him
to be a lucky one, and which he resolved to put into immediate
Execution: Alas! *said he*, to the Maid, do you not know your
Mistress is Mad!—you do not certainly regard any Thing she
says of late? Mad, Sir! *cry'd she*, not well knowing whether he
spoke in earnest or not, till he endeavour'd to assure her in these
Words; Aye, *resum'd he*, my poor Niece was a few days ago seiz'd
with a most violent Frenzy, I had hope would have gone off,
and therefore spoke not of it to any body; but I find the Distemper increases upon her, and that so strongly, that it will be
dangerous to let her go loose about the House—I know not but
in some sudden Starts she may attempt to do some mischief
either to herself or others. Oh! my Stars! Mad! *cry'd she again*;
nay, she is in a strange Humour now; I beseech you Sir, give me
my Discharge, for I shall be afraid of coming near her. You shall
not need, *answer'd he*, I will have her lock'd into her Chamber

immediately; in the mean time I would not have you appear before her, but instead of going to provide a Lodging for her, order one of the Footmen to bring a Smith, that her Windows may be barr'd, for 'tis not Impossible but when she finds she is restrain'd in her Humour she may offer to throw herself out. Very true, Sir! *said she*, one cannot be too secure. With these Words she went out of the Room to do as she was commanded. And *Horatio* admir'd the Subtilty of his Father in finding out an Expedient which would either oblige her to comply with their Desires, or give them, as being next of kin, the Possession of her Estate, her being represented as a Lunatick, and consequently incapable of managing it.

Annilia, who after she had finish'd the little Affairs she had been about, waited with Impatience for the return of her Woman, was strangely surpriz'd when she saw *Giraldo* with *Horatio* come into her Chamber; she imagin'd not, that after the Resolution she had express'd, she should be troubled with any further Importunities from them, at least for some time: Well, Niece, said the former of them, have you considered on what I have said, or do you still persevere in Obstinacy? Yes, *answer'd she*, my Resolution yet holds firm never to confer greater Power in those Hands who have made so ill a Use of what they have already. You talk as if you could restrain it, *resum'd he*; but come into my Closet, I will give you leave to peruse the Writings of your Estate, and the last Testament of your dying Father; then you will be convinced how far his Confidence rely'd on me for the Director of your Actions. *Annilia* comply'd with this Request, glad to look over Particulars which as yet she had known but by the Report of others.

They detain'd her here in reading the Papers, and disputing on the meaning of the Contents of them, till word was brought to *Giraldo* that every thing was ready; and then breaking off the Conversation, they suffer'd her to depart, who by this time not doubting but her Woman was come back, went directly to her Chamber, where she no sooner enter'd, than to her great Amazement she saw the Windows with Iron-Bars grated like a Prison; she was turning back with a design to ask the meaning of it, and to enquire after the Person she had sent, when her cruel Uncle, who was close behind her, shut the Door upon her, and having lock'd it fast, put the Key in his Pocket.

It would be needless to go about to describe the Violence of her Rage at finding herself thus confin'd; the Reader will easily believe, that on so just a Provocation, Passion must arrive at the greatest pitch imaginable; she rang her Bell, she stamp'd with her Feet, she call'd, but all in vain, none durst come to her Relief; and possess'd first by what the Wench had said, and which after both their Masters confirmed; none of the Family even wish'd her Liberty, but thought her Imprisonment the effect of Care.

In this manner did she continue several days, none coming near her but *Giraldo*, who was himself the Bearer of what Food or other Necessaries she was allow'd. In every one of these Visits he pressed her to Compliance, still assuring her that she must hope for Liberty on no other Terms than by becoming the Bride of *Horatio*, and mingling with his Persuasions, Menaces of a worse Treatment than that which she at present experienced, if she persisted to refuse. But in this she show'd a Strength of Mind, and an unshaken Constancy, infinitely beyond what could be expected from her Years, or indeed what we have many Examples of in the other Sex; and replying to what he said with a dauntless Fortitude, and noble Boldness, which would have struck into any Heart, that was not wholly render'd inexorable by Avarice, told him, that not only to procure her Liberty, but to preserve her Life, she would never yield to be the Wife of a Man, who had consented to use her with so unexampled a Barbarity; and bid him invent means to increase her Sufferings as far beyond what they were, as he either could or dare; the Pleasure it gave her to let him see they were in vain, would more than compensate for the Pain.

Whenever she upbraided him with his abusing the Names of Uncle and Guardian, he said that she had no reason to accuse him of any avaritious Views; for if it were so, he had the same Pretensions to her Estate while suppos'd a Lunatick, as his Son

would have if made her Husband;[10] and that as all the measures
he had taken were only to give her Happiness, she had only her
own perverse Humour to condemn, if she were not so. But this
way of Reasoning having no effect on her, and that every day
her Resolution rather grew stronger than any way abated, the
Impossibility there appear'd of bringing her to his Terms, together with the Fear that by some Accident it might probably
come to be discover'd, that she was not as he had represented
her, made him think of removing her to one of those Houses
which are prepared on purpose for the Reception of Persons
disorder'd in their Senses:[11] he had often been told, that for a
good Gratification, the Doors would be open as well for those
whom it was necessary, for the Interest of their Friends, to be
made Mad, as for those who were so in reality, and resolved
now to make the Experiment. He had recourse to one at a small
distance from the City where he lived, and found the Master of
it as compliable to his Desires as he could have hoped. Every
thing being agreed upon between them, all the Difficulty lay in
removing her; for *Giraldo* was unwilling it should be done in a
publick manner, because he thought it improper that any Person beside himself and Son, should know to what Place she was
convey'd: It was therefore concluded on, that at the Dead of
Night, a Hackney Coach[12] should be brought to the Door, into
which she should be put, under the Guard of two or three Men
belonging to the Keeper of the Lunaticks.

The Hour appointed for the Execution of this Enterprize

---

[10]*same Pretensions to her Estate. . .if made her Husband* Lunatics and women were
not allowed to possess their own estates. By declaring Annilia mad, Giraldo has
as much control over her fortune as Horatio would if she were married to him.
Haywood draws a parallel between the state of madness and marriage, empha-
sizing the disempowerment of women.

[11]*those Houses. . .Persons disorder'd in their Senses* With exceptions such as Bethle-
hem Hospital (Bedlam) and St. Luke's Hospital (est. 1751), lunatic asylums
were privately owned and managed. As Haywood implies here, inmates could
be incarcerated at the capricious desire of their relatives.

[12]*Hackney Coach* a four-wheeled coach, drawn by two horses, and seated for
six persons, kept for hire (OED).

being near at hand, *Giraldo* order'd all his Family to retire to their Beds, except one Servant, in whom he plac'd great Confidence, and was the same who occasion'd his discovering the Correspondence between *Marathon* and *Annilia*, by giving him Intelligence out of what place he had seen *Osepha* come. The unhappy Niece of this barbarous Man was compell'd to rise out of her Bed, where she was sleeping as secure as her Discontents and Fears would let her, and oblig'd to put on her Clothes at that unseasonable Hour; not that she would have done it at his request, but the appearance of all those ill-look'd Fellows in her Chamber, (he having without any regard to Decency, or the Modesty of her Sex, brought them to her Bed-side) made her, with all the haste she could, throw on a loose Night-Gown, which she had no sooner done, than like a Lamb among a Herd of Wolves, she was seiz'd by these inhuman Ruffians; and some stopping her Mouth, and threatning her if she attempted to resist; and another taking hold of her, she was rather dragg'd than carry'd down Stairs, and thrust into the Coach, where the three Keepers immediately crowding in, render'd frustrate all the faint Hopes she had conceived of escaping.

She saw little of the Horrors of her Prison that Night, every Wretch, whom either the Malice of their false Friends, or the Misfortune of their own Distemper, had brought there, being close lock'd into their several Apartments; and all the Family, who profited by their Misery, retir'd to Bed, except two Women-Servants, who humouring this new Guest in all the Extravagancies her Wrongs enforc'd her to utter, made her know that it was to a Mad-House she was brought, and that they took her for one labouring under that unhappy Circumstance. They compelled her to go into a Bed they had prepar'd for her, but 'tis not to be imagin'd she could admit the Approach of Sleep that Night; and earlier than the Day, was she disturb'd with Sounds, which struck so great a Dread into her, that nothing is more strange, than that she did not die with the Fright, or fall indeed into that Disorder of which she was accus'd — The rattling of Chains, the Shrieks of those severely treated by their barbarous Keepers, mingled with Curses, Oaths, and the most blasphemous Imprecations, did from one quarter of the House shock her tormented Ears; while from another, Howlings like that of Dogs, Shoutings, Roarings, Prayers, Preaching, Curses, Singing, Crying, promiscuously join'd to make a Chaos of the most horrible Confusion: but the Violence of this Uproar continued not long, it being only occasion'd by the first Entrance of the Keepers into the Cells of those Wretches who were really Lunatick, and had, for the Addition of their Anguish, so much Remains of Sense, as to know what they were to suffer at the Approach of these inhuman Creatures, who never came to bring them fresh Straw, or that poor Pittance of Food allowed for the Support of their miserable Lives; but they saluted them with Stripes[13] in a manner so cruel, as if they delighted in inflicting Pain, excusing themselves in this Barbarity, by saying that there was a necessity to keep them in awe; as if Chains, and Nakedness, and the small Portion of wretched Sustenance they suffer'd them to take, was not sufficient to humble their Fellow-Creature. Besides, what is there to be feared from those helpless Objects of Compassion, who being Hand-cuffed, and the Fetters on their Legs fast bolted into the Floor, can stir no farther than the length of their Chain! Yet with Barbarity do these pityless Monsters exert the Power they have over them, that whoever is witness of it, would imagine they were rather placed there for the Punishment of some Capital Crime, for which Law has provided no sufficient Torture, than for the Cure of a Disease, by their nearest and dearest Relations.[14]

To find herself in such a Place, and that it was made so secure by Locks, by Bolts, and Bars, that all Thoughts of making her

---

[13]*Stripes* strokes or lashes with a whip or scourge (OED).

[14]*pityless Monsters exert the Power* Medical therapy for mad patients included not only what Haywood describes here but bleedings, the administering of violent emetics and purgatives, as well as medicine to encourage perspiration, and mercury to produce excessive saliva. For further details on the treatment of patients in eighteenth-century private madhouses, see Allan Ingram's *The Madhouse of Language: Writing and Reading Madness in the Eighteenth-Century* (London, 1991), especially pp. 40–43 which describe the water therapy of one Dr. Patrick Blair.

Escape would be in vain, was enough to have made a Woman
less endued with Fortitude, consent to any thing for her Enlargement; but she, in the midst of her Distress, justly reflecting
that those who could be capable of using her in this inhuman
manner to force her to a Compliance, might hereafter, when
satiated with Enjoyment, or the least Disgust, have recourse to
the same means to get rid of her, as now they took to gain her,
resolved rather to die, than yield to put a greater power into the
hands of Persons, who had made so detestable a Use of what
they had already. The Remembrance of *Marathon*, and the Impossibility there appear'd of ever seeing that dear Man again,
was a considerable Augmentation of her Sorrows; she doubted
not but she was confined for Life, and being deprived of all
means of sending to him, or letting him know what 'twas she
suffer'd for his sake, made the Tears stream from her fair Eyes,
when nothing else could call them forth. She continued in this
dejected State for about fourteen Weeks, without being able to
entertain the least hope of Relief; in all which time *Giraldo* had
visited her but twice, the Pressures he now made her in behalf
of his Son were so faint, that it was easy for her to perceive, he
was indifferent whether she comply'd or not, which confirmed
that Opinion she before had but too much reason to harbour,
that it was for her Wealth alone that he had seem'd so desirous
of engaging her; and tho' it was infinite Trouble to her to think
that they enjoy'd that, yet the Satisfaction it gave her to reflect
that he had not her Person also, very much alleviated the
Pain. — Some kind Turn of Fate, *said she to herself*, may disclose
the villainous Practices of these abandon'd Wretches, and put
me in possession of my own; but had the Marriage Ceremony
past, all had been irrevocably lost, and I undone beyond all
hope of Vengeance or Redress.

In this Condition, beguiling as much as possible her miserable Hours, let us leave her for a time, and see in what manner
her Lover resented this sudden Alteration in his Fortune.
Osephas had no sooner been discharg'd by *Giraldo*, than he went
to the Colonel, acquainting him with the Truth of all that happen'd to him: that Gentleman was too generous to let him suffer

for having been faithful to him, and immediately receiv'd him into his Service. He found so much difference between these two Masters, that the Goodness of the latter engaged him in Ties more strong than those of Duty; there was nothing he would not have done to procure him Satisfaction: and finding he prodigiously lamented the Loss of *Annilia*, he kept his Brain on a continual Rack[15] for some Invention to restore her to him. In the Neighbourhood of *Giraldo* he was inform'd of the Report of her being Lunatick, and soon after that she was remov'd from the House of her Uncle, but to what Place, none knew. This Intelligence render'd the impatient *Marathon* almost in the same Condition in reality, as she was feign'd to be: He went to every one of those Receptacles of unhappy Persons, and enquir'd for *Annilia* in a manner which might have made him pass for one as little in his Senses as any they had the Charge of; for certainly had he at that time been master of his Reason, it would have inform'd him how little probability there was, that the way he took should succeed.

Being convinc'd of his Error, he would have had recourse to Law, and compell'd *Giraldo* to satisfy the World in what manner he had dispos'd of his Niece; but found this would be as ineffectual as the other Measures he had taken. He had but a slender Fortune of his own; *Giraldo* was at present in possession of a very great one, and by that means was better enabled to maintain the Wrong he had done, than the other was to oblige him to acknowledge it. Besides, *Annilia* had no Kindred living so near to her as *Giraldo* and *Horatio*, and the more distant ones evaded being concern'd with a Stranger, against Persons who they knew not but might have reason for what they did, or if they had not, every one cry'd it was none of his business; and the disconsolate Colonel was enforc'd to let this Project drop, since it was wholly impossible for him to carry it on alone. He was several times about sending a Challenge to *Horatio*, flattering

---

[15]*Rack* an instrument of torture formerly in use, consisting (usually) of a frame having a roller at each end; the victim was fastened to these by the wrists and ankles, and had the joints of his limbs stretched by their rotation (OED).

himself with the hope, that if he had the better, his Antagonist would be glad to purchase his Life at the Expence of the Secret; but *Osephas*, as often as he heard him mention it, endeavour'd to avert his Design. Ah Sir! I beseech you, *would he say to him*, give over such Thoughts; consider there are many Chances against that one you wish: should you fall by the Sword of *Horatio*, poor *Annilia* would be then left defenceless indeed; or should your juster Arm prevail, and punish all the Crimes of that vile Man, by giving him his Death, you know how severe our Law is against Duellists,[16] much less can the Challenger be thought to merit Mercy; the Judges, partial to the Statute, will not consider the Greatness of the Provocation, your Merits, or your Rival's Baseness — Either way therefore you rob *Annilia* of the only Friend, who either can or will attempt any thing for her Delivery; I beg you then to wait a little with Patience — You know not what Discoveries Time and Industry may bring about. By these kind of Arguments he brought him to delay his Purpose for some time, but would not much longer have been able to restrain his Impatience, had not an Accident happen'd, which gave them a View of accomplishing the Freedom of *Annilia* by a way less fatal. *Osephas* had heard, that the Maid who formerly waited on *Annilia*, was gone from the House of *Giraldo*; he made it his business therefore to inform himself of what place she now was, which having done, he resolv'd to visit her, imagining that she might be able to tell him where it was that her Mistress was convey'd: but not finding her at home, and hearing that she was expected in an hour, he went to pass that time in the Fields, which were but at the end of that Street in which she lived. He had not walked many Turns, before he saw a

---

[16]*Law. . .against Duellists* "in the case of deliberate duelling,. . .both parties meet avowedly with an intent to murder: thinking it their duty, as gentlemen, and claiming it as their right, to wanton with their own lives and those of their fellow creatures; without any warrant or authority from any power either divine or human, but in direct contradiction to the laws both of God and man: and therefore the law has justly fixed the crime and punishment of murder, on them, and on their seconds also" (Blackstone, Bk. IV, chap. 14, 199). The penalty for murder was death by hanging.

Hackney-Coach, with only one Gentleman in it, cross the Road, and turn down a By-Path, which he knew led to one of those Mad-Houses, where his Master had been to enquire for *Annilia*; tho' he was at a great distance, it came into his head that the Person he saw in that Coach was *Giraldo*; and resolving to be certain, ran with all the speed he could the way it had gone: He arriv'd timely enough to see him alight at the Gate, and go in, for it was indeed no other than *Giraldo*, who was then going to put the Question to his unfortunate Niece in one of those Visits already mention'd. *Osephas* made now no doubt, but that it was in this House *Annilia* was confined; and instead of prosecuting his Design of renewing his Acquaintance with the Maid, ran directly home, and gave his Master an Account of what he had seen. Never was Man more transported than was he at this Intelligence; he look'd on the knowledge in what place she was, as one very considerable step, as indeed it was, to the getting her out: and since Fortune had favour'd him thus far, was now in hope she would not turn her back, till he had entirely accomplish'd his Intent. He found, however, that it must be by Subtilty, and not Force, that he must become Master of his Wishes, and therefore carefully conceal'd, as did *Osephas* also, the Discovery they had made: After having pass'd two or three days in fruitless Projections, Love, ever ready in Stratagems, furnish'd the assiduous *Marathon* with one, which having communicated to *Osephas*, he agreed with him that there was nothing in it impracticable, or very difficult; it was, that he should counterfeit Madness,[17] and get some Person of his Acquaintance to recommend him as a Patient of Note, and who they would be well recompensed for taking care of, and that *Osephas* having chang'd his Livery, should also attend him there. 'Tis possible, *said the Colonel*, that *Giraldo* may not often come there; or if he does, it will be easy for you to avoid letting him see you: — The

---

[17]*counterfeit Madness* A similar plot is used by Middleton in his 1622 play *The Changeling*. In that play, Franciscus pretends madness in order to get close to Isabella, the wife of the jealous Alibius. She has been incarcerated by her husband to prevent her cuckolding him.

Confinement will not be long, for if I once get on the Inside of the House, I do not doubt but to have my dear *Annilia* out in a short time.

This Design was no sooner concluded on, than they went about the Execution of it. *Marathon* sent for a young Gentleman in whom he could confide, to whom he communicated the whole Affair, and intreated his Assistance so far as to make an Agreement for him with the Keeper of the Lunaticks. *Olario*, for that was his Name, readily consented to do as his Friend desir'd, and took Coach immediately for the Mad-House, where giving a small Present in hand, and an Assurance of a sufficient Gratification hereafter; it was presently agreed upon, that his Friend should be receiv'd whenever he came: They made some difficulty of admitting a Servant, not being willing to have any Person at liberty to inspect into their Behaviour, to those who were confin'd; but *Olario* insisting on it, it was at last consented to.

Olario having thus far succeeded, came back to his Friend, who in the mean time had been providing himself of a Habit very different from what he was accustom'd to wear, justly judging it improper to appear the same Man who had been to demand *Annilia*, and threaten'd them that detain'd her; this being one of those Houses, which in his Search for her, he had visited in this manner. But he now seem'd so much another, that there was not a possibility for Persons who had seen him but once, to know him again: He was in a very rich Suit of Clothes embroider'd with Gold, a white Feather in his Hat, and a fine Tassel of *Barbary* Work hanging at his Sword: He had now none of these Ornaments, but appear'd like a plain Country Gentleman, for such he pass'd for; and his Name was chang'd from that of *Marathon* to *Lovemore*, as was that of *Osephas* to *Andrew*, who was also habited like one of those Servants who do the Offices of Butler, Groom, Valet, and Footman. Thus equip'd did Olario return with them to the Region of Lunacy, and having seen the pretended Patient to his Chamber, and order'd him to be well look'd after, left him with *Osephas*, now *Andrew*, in their voluntary Imprisonment.

Now were they to apply themselves to their several Tasks; the Colonel, whom we must now call *Lovemore*, had nothing to do but to fetch heavy Sighs, walk with his Arms a-cross, now and then beat his Breast, and some other such like Tokens of Despair;[18] for *Olario* had told them it was a melancholy Madness of which he was possess'd. But the Business of *Andrew* was to create an Intimacy with the Servants, and in particular with the Maids, pry about the House, and discover in what part of it *Annilia* was kept, and who it was that had the Charge of her Room. Both succeeded so well, that there was not the least doubt but that one was as really mad as 'twas possible to be; and that the other was the most diligent and best-natur'd Servant in the World. Had *Andrew* been dispos'd to marry, he might have had his Choice of any of the Maids in that House; but having found out in which Chamber *Annilia* was lodg'd, he made his whole Court to her who attended that Lady: and by following her up and down Stairs, and wherever she went, under the pretence of Love, had frequently an opportunity of seeing the lovely Object of his Master's Affections: Having assur'd him of the Certainty of her being there, he was commanded to bring Paper, Pen, and Ink, which he having done unknown to the Keepers, who never permit the Use to their Patients, he wrote this short but passionate Billet to her.

To the most Injur'd, but most Divine
ANNILIA.

I Will not upbraid you, that you rejected the Counsels of your faithful Adorer, nor endeavour to aggrandize my Services, by setting forth the Difficulties I met with in my Search of you — 'Tis sufficient that I now have found you — that I have contrived the means of your Escape from this vile Prison — and think myself the happiest of Mortals, in having been able to baffle all the Plots your Enemies had laid to involve you in a lasting Misery — I am near you, most adorable *Annilia*, but have not yet

---

[18]*heavy Sighs,. . .Despair* "Lovemore's" melancholy madness is reminiscent of Hamlet's behaviour to Ophelia (2.1. 75-97).

the power to throw myself beneath your Feet—shortly shall I enjoy that boundless Blessing, yet could I not refrain sending this Harbinger of my Approach, and preparing you for that Deliverance you are shortly to receive from

Your transported Slave,

MARATHON.

This he committed to the Care of the subtile *Osephas* to deliver to her; but having receiv'd it, he was more than half afraid he should not be able to execute his Commission. The Maid who had the Care of her Room, had receiv'd so strict a Charge from her Master to suffer no Person to come to the Speech of her, that he found it utterly impossible, and would not therefore attempt it. As he was walking in the Gardens, vex'd at the ill Success of his Design, he saw a little Boy shooting at the Birds with a Bow and Arrow; he made a pretence to send the Child on some Errand, and taking his Arrows, fix'd the Letter to one of them, and being a pretty good Marksman, shot it in between the Iron Bars of *Annilia's* Window, her Casement happening fortunately to be left open.

That disconsolate Lady was sitting in an Arm'd-Chair, at some distance from the Window, when the Arrow fell directly at her feet, which believing sent by some Child, her Good-Nature made her take it up, with an Intent to throw it back, unwilling to deprive the innocent Shooter of his Diversion; but the Surprize which seiz'd her Soul at sight of the Paper annex'd to it, and her perfect Knowledge of the dear Characters which compos'd the Superscription, can no way be conceiv'd but by a Person equally enamour'd, equally distress'd like her—But when she had examin'd the Contents, Wonder gave place to Joy, and 'tis difficult to say whether the Hopes of her Deliverance, or the Thoughts that it was to *Marathon* she was indebted for it, gave her the greatest Satisfaction. As soon as she could recall her Spirits from that Absence of Mind, which the first Emotions of Amazement had involved her in, she ran to the Window, imagining that *Marathon* himself might possibly be there. *Osephas*, who guess'd to what her Curiosity might excite her, continued walking, and when he perceiv'd she look'd toward him, made a reverend Bow, and then went hastily away, testifying by his Motions, that they must proceed with Caution. In spite of the Alteration which his Change of Habit had made in him, she presently knew this faithful Servant, but by what means he had gain'd Entrance into that House, could not be able to comprehend. The Sight of him, however, confirming her that there was something in hand for her Deliverance, settled a Contentment in her Mind, which for many Weeks had been a Stranger there; and she bore her Captivity with Patience, expecting every hour to be released, and by the Man to whom of all the World she most desired to be obliged.

Nor was it many days after the Receipt of this Letter, that the industrious Contrivers of her Enlargement suffer'd her to continue in suspence: and the means they made use of to accomplish that Purpose, were as follows.

Osephas had observ'd that all day the Keys were left on the outside of the Doors of those Rooms which inclosed the Patients, for the Convenience of the Servants going backward and forward with their Allowance of Food and other Necessaries, but that at night they were all deliver'd to the Master of the House; on which he watch'd an opportunity of taking that of *Annilia*'s Prison, and making the Impression of it in Wax, which, having the Liberty of going out whenever he pleased, he carry'd to a Smith of his Acquaintance, and got one made exactly like it. The Colonel having try'd the Lock of his own Door, found he could push it back without any noise. The Difficulty now lay how to get out of the House Door, that Key never being left in the Lock, and also how *Osephas*, who lay with one of the Under-Keepers, should leave his Bed without Suspicion; but as there was no possibility of escaping without some Hazard, he carry'd this Fellow to a House of Entertainment, where making him pretty merry with variety of Liquors, he brought a Bottle home with him, of a sort which he perceiv'd the other seem'd to like the best of any, saying, they would drink that together when the Family were in bed; which he, thinking all was safe, gladly comply'd with: and the watchful Osephas ply'd him so home, that he at last fell, what they call dead drunk, upon the Bed, on which they both were sitting. As soon as he perceiv'd him fast, he went softly to his Master's Chamber, who expecting him about this Hour, had already push'd back the Lock—they pass'd no time in Talk, but went directly to *Annilia*'s, and making use of the Key which *Osephas* had procur'd, enter'd, and found that Lady in a sound Sleep. In spite of the Danger they were in of Discovery, the amorous Colonel could not forbear wasting some moments in gazing on the adorable Object of his Affections, thus unseen by her; and perhaps had continued longer in that tender Resvery, had not *Osephas* reminded him, that in indulging a present Delight, he might possibly incur eternal Grief; he was at last prevail'd on to wake her, which he did, by gently kissing her Hand: Had not the Letter prepared her for an Encounter of this nature, the sight of two Men in her Chamber at such an hour, might probably have thrown her into a Surprize fatal to their Designs, and her own Wishes. Be not frighted, *said he to her, as soon as she began to open her Eyes*, 'tis *Marathon*, your ever-faithful Slave, who comes to deliver you from this Scene of Woe, of Treachery and Injustice—all things are ready, haste, my Angel, that I may conduct you hence. *Marathon! cry'd she*, is it possible? All things are so, *reply'd he*, to Love like mine; but 'tis not now a Season to relate by what means I am the happy Instrument of Heaven for your Release—be speedy in preparing yourself to go—I will retire with *Osephas* into the Gallery while you put on your Clothes. He staid not for her Answer, but immediately went out of the Room; and 'tis not to be doubted but she made as much haste in doing as she was desir'd, as the Surprize she was in, and the Darkness of the Night, would give her leave to do; for they durst bring no Light with them, for fear of a Discovery.

She had never any other Clothes sent her, than those in which she came; therefore in the same loose Dress in which she was forced thither, did she escape. Being ready in a very few minutes, she came out of the Room, where *Marathon* receiv'd her in his Arms, and after recompensing himself for the pains he had taken by a passionate Embrace, which she thought not too great a Favour to be permitted to one, who had done so much to prove his Love and Fidelity; they both follow'd *Osephas*, who knowing the way of the House much better than those who had never traversed it, but when they were led into the Chambers allotted for them, was their Guide and Conductor. It being impossible to get the great Door of the House open, he went into a Parlour, which, the Lunaticks never being suffer'd to enter, had no Iron Bars to the Windows; he therefore open'd the Shutters, and drawing up the Sashes, got easily out, as did *Marathon*, and from thence lifted the trembling *Annilia* in his Arms. Being all safe in the Court-yard, but a great Chain being cross the Gate, it was thought dangerous to attempt to force that Lock, which could not be done without Noise; it seem'd therefore more advisable to climb the Wall, which, tho' it was very high, the Men could do with ease, all the difficulty lay in getting the Lady over, but *Osephas* contrived it in this manner: He persuaded his Master to go first, and then by kneeling down, and making *Annilia* set her Feet upon his Shoulders, when he rose up, and stood upright, she could with her Hands reach the Top of the Wall; and scrupling no Danger which gave her hopes of Freedom, she consented to it, and having a moment or two upon it to take a breath, she ventur'd to jump down on the other side, where the transported *Marathon* caught her safely in his Arms: the nimble *Osephas* was after her in a minute; and all hastily turning their Backs on that detested House, rested not till they arrived at the Colonel's Lodgings. It was here that they had that Blessing, which none but Lovers know, of testifying their mutual Tenderness by a thousand Vows and soft Protestations of an inviolable Affection. But what transported him almost beyond his Reason, was, that she told him that as soon as Morning arrived, to which it was now but a few Hours, she would put it past the power of the whole World to separate them for the future, by becoming his by those Tyes, which are not to be dissolv'd but by Death.

Nor did she fail in the Performance of that Promise, which not only her Inclinations, but her Reputation also, as it was with him that she had escaped from the Mad-House, induc'd

61

her to make him. Soon therefore as *Aurora*'s Beams[19] proclaim'd the coming Day, she sent *Osephas* to some of those with whom she had been most intimate of both Sexes, desiring them to come to her immediately at the Place where she then was, bidding him tell them they should hear a Story full of Wonder. The Summons being, either out of Love or Curiosity, readily obey'd, she related to them the whole of her Adventure, and the unexampled Barbarity of her Uncle; and then intreated them to accompany her to the next Church, and see her dispose of herself to the Man to whom she owed her Redemption, and who, she said, by that Service, if by no other, had more than merited her. The Ladies observing her Habit, and having been inform'd by her, that her Uncle had suffer'd her to have no other to put on, would have sent for some of theirs; but she would not consent to it, only accepting a Hood and Scarf from one of them, saying merrily, her Bridegroom would not like her the less hereafter, for being ill-dress'd on her Wedding-Day.

The Ceremony of Marriage over, all who were present at it, by her Desire accompany'd her to the House of *Giraldo*, and gave a Surprize to that inhuman Man, proportionable to the Crime he had been guilty of. *Annilia* in mild Terms reproach'd him with his Usage of her, and demanded the Writings of her Estate, Which, *said she*, are now the Right of my Husband, *pointing to Colonel* Marathon. I shall do nothing, *reply'd he sullenly*, till I have had the Advice of my Lawyer; then you shall hear further from me. Look that it be speedy, *said the Colonel*, or you must expect to hear from me in a manner you will have no reason to be pleased with. They had no further Discourse, the new-wedded Pair were as little able to brook the Sight of him, as he was pleased with theirs; and the whole Company adjourn'd to a House of *Marathon*'s Acquaintance, where they had an Entertainment suitable to the Day: after which, he, with his dear *Annilia*, retired to his own Lodgings, and there was in possession of the Joy he had so long languished for.

---

[19]*Aurora's Beams* Aurora was the goddess of the dawn; the phrase figuratively refers to the rising light of morning (OED).

Some Days being elaps'd, and *Giraldo* not sending according to his Promise, the Colonel gave orders to an Attorney to take such measures as should compel him to do justice: on which he offer'd to come to Terms of Accommodation; the Proposals he made, were to deliver up the Writings, Jewels, Plate, and all other Things belonging to *Annilia*, if she would consent to give him a Release for what he had receiv'd of the yearly Revenue since the Decease of her Father: to which, in consideration of the Tenderness with which he had treated her, till the Time of his going about to force her to a Marriage with his Son; and to avoid the Trouble and Fatigue which attends a Suit in Law, she readily comply'd; and by delivering all, as soon as she receiv'd it, into the hands of *Marathon*, confirm'd him of the good Opinion she had of him.

The ill Success of *Giraldo*'s Designs, together with the Shame and Disreputation, which the Discovery of his late Proceedings had drawn on him, threw him into a Fever, of which he died, when he was not many Years pass'd that Age, which is call'd the Prime. His Son *Horatio* being accounted equally blameable, not able to endure the Reproaches which were daily made him, even by Persons the least interested in the Affair, left the Kingdom, and has not since been heard of. May all such base Designers meet the same Fate; let them in foreign Lands wander unfriended, unregarded, fit Society only for Beasts of Prey; while the Constant and Sincere meet with a Recompence proportion'd to their Merit, happy in themselves, and triumphant over those who seek or to detract, or to prejudice them.

F I N I S.

THE

CITY JILT;

OR, THE

Alderman turn'd Beau:

A SECRET

HISTORY.

Virtue now, nor noble Blood,

Nor Wit by Love is understood;

Gold alone does Passion move:

Gold monopolizes Love.

COWLEY.[20]

[20]The epigraph is taken from Abraham Cowley's *Anacreontiques; or, Some Copies of Verses, translated Paraphrastically out of* ANACREON, VII. "Gold" (Grosart).

THE Alderman turn'ed B E A U

GLICERA was the Daughter of an eminent Tradesman, the Reputation of whose Riches drew a greater Number of Admirers to his House, than the Beauty of his fair Daughter's Person; tho' she was really one of the most lovely and accomplished Women of the Age. The most favour'd of all who made Pretensions to her, was young *Melladore*, the Son of a near Neighbour; he was handsome, witty, well made, and seem'd to have an infinity of Affection for her. With all these Endowments therefore, join'd to an Equality of Birth and Fortune, 'tis not to be wondered at that he was well received by the Father of *Glicera*, as well as by herself. Nothing happening between them but what is common to Persons in the Circumstances they were, I shall pass over in silence the Days of their Courtship, and only say that their mutual Affection encreasing the more they knew each other's Temper; and every thing being agreed on by the Relations on both sides, a Day was appointed for the Celebration of their Nuptials.

Now did this enamour'd Pair think of nothing but approaching Joys, all the delightful Visions with which the God of Love deludes his Votaries, play'd before their Eyes, and formed a thousand Day-dreams of an imaginary Heaven of Pleasure — with equal Ardour, equal Languishment did both long for the happy Minute which was to crown their Loves, — the impatient Youth with fierce and vigorous Wishes burn'd, the tender Maid in soft Desires dissolv'd. — Alas! she knew not yet the meaning of those tumultuous Agitations, which at every Kiss and fond Embrace she received from the amorous *Melladore*, made her Heart flutter with disordered Beatings, the Blood flow fast through each throbbing Vein, and a wild Mixture of Delight and Pain invade her every Faculty: — But he, more experienced, was not ignorant what it was, for which he sigh'd; scarce cou'd he refrain taking those Advantages which her Innocence and Love afforded him, to make him Master of the supremest Bliss that Passion can demand, or Beauty yield; and the Agonies of suppress'd Desire would sometimes rise to such a Height, that nothing but the extremest Respect could have enabled him to endure them, rather than be guilty of the least Action which might shock the timorous Bashfulness of her virgin Soul.

In this Position were their Hearts, while those necessary Preparations were about, for the rendering magnificent that Ceremony which was to put an end to the Lover's Impatience, and the Virgin's Scruples. There now wanted but one Day of that which was to be the happy one, and 'tis difficult to say whether *Melladore*, or his intended Bride, felt the greater Satisfaction at the near Approach. But to what Vicissitudes are the Transports of Lovers incident! The Father of *Glicera* was taken suddenly ill, and that with so much Violence, that in a few hours time his Life was despaired of; Night brought with it an encrease of his Distemper, nor did the Morning afford any Abatement; not all the Prescriptions of the best Physicians, who were sent for on his first finding himself disordered, had the least Effect on him; and at the close of the second Day he paid that Debt to Nature, to which all who live must submit.

Here was now a sad Change in the Affairs of *Glicera*, her bridal Ornaments were exchanged for mournful Black; and at the time when she expected to have received the Gratulations of her Friends for her happy Nuptials, she had only the Consolations of them to regard. The Society of her dear *Melladore* was however a considerable Alleviation to her Sorrows, and as he scarce ever left her but in those Hours in which Decency obliged him to retire, he easily persuaded her to a Forgetfulness of *the Dead*, in the Comforts of *the Living*; and if Fate exacted the Life of one, she thought it yet a less terrible Misfortune to lose her *Father* than a *Lover* who was so dear to her, and by whom she believed herself so sincerely and tenderly belov'd, that she should know no want of any other Friend. Ah! how little is Youth sensible of what it owes to Age, and how far are we unable to conceive what is due to the Care of a tender Parent, or how greatly we suffer in the loss of such a one! But soon was this fond Maid made sensible of her Error; soon, alas! did sad Experience convince her of the Difference between natural Affection and the Vows of Passion.

Many People, who while they live make a very great Show, when once Death exposes to the World the truth of their Circumstances, are found vastly inferior to what their Appearance had promised: At least it here so happened, the Father of *Glicera*, reputed one of the richest Citizens of his Time, left behind him little more than would serve to defray the Expences of his Funeral, and pay the Debts he had contracted; and the fair Subject of this little History, instead of a hundred thousand Crowns,[21] which was the least that was expected for her Portion, had scarce sufficient left her to maintain her one Year in the manner she had been accustomed to live. *Melladore*, however, had enough for both; and fully depending on his Love and Constancy, she regarded not this Fall from her high-rais'd Hopes, nor once imagined that the Loss of her Wealth would also make her lose his Heart: for this reason, as well as that her Youth had not yet learned Hypocrisy, and scorn'd the Baseness of a Lye, she endeavoured not to conceal the reality of her Affairs, but frankly let him know that her Love and Virtue were her only Dower. They were sitting in an Arbour at the end of the Garden, so shadow'd o'er with Trees, that scarce could the Sun's Beams at the height of Noon penetrate the Gloom, much less those of the pale Moon, who then shone but with faint and sickly Fires, when first she related to him this surprizing News; so that unhappily for her she perceived not the shock her Words had given him, nor the Disorders which that moment overspread his alter'd Countenance: and being far from guessing at his Thoughts, prosecuted her Discourse without expecting any Reply from him till he had time

---

[21] *a hundred thousand Crowns* £25,000

enough to recollect himself, and have recourse to Dissimulation. And then he did not fail to tell her, that her adorable
Person was of itself a Treasure infinitely beyond his Merit, —
that he look'd on her as a Blessing sent from Heaven to make
him the happiest of his Sex — that he rather rejoiced than the
contrary, at this Opportunity to prove the Disinterestedness of
his Affection, — and a thousand such like Expressions of Tenderness and Truth, which she hesitated not if she should believe, because she wish'd it so, and had before set down in her
own Heart for Truth, all that he now professed.

So artfully did he deceive, that for many Weeks she had not
the least reason to suspect, but that as soon as Decency for the
Death of her Father would permit,[22] she should become his
Wife: But vastly different now were his Designs, the real Love
he had was to the Wealth of which he expected she would be
possess'd; but that being lost, his Passion also vanish'd, and left
behind it only that part of Desire which tends to Enjoyment; —
the nobler Inclinations all were fled, and brutal Appetite alone
remained: — In an unguarded Hour, when most he found her
melted by his Pressures, and wholly incapable of repelling his
amorous Efforts, did he attack her with all the ruinous Force of
fatal Passion — He told her, that since their Hearts were united
too firmly to be ever separated, 'twere most unjust to themselves and the soft Languishments which both confess'd, to
make their Bodies observe a cruel Distance: — That Caution
between them now was needless, — and tho' in regard to Custom, and that Decorum which enslaves the World, the Ceremony which was to authorize Possession had not yet passed; yet
might they in secret indulge those Wishes to which Marriage
hereafter would give a Sanction. — By such kind of Arguments,
accompanied with unnumber'd Vows, Sighs, Tears, and Implo-

---

[22]*Decency for the Death of her Father would permit* I have been unable to find any
specific or "decent" mourning period for a father; however, eighteenth-century
widows were expected to keep to their house for six weeks (Ashton, 1:59). It
would be reasonable to assume that a parent's death would warrant less than
this period, but Glicera seems to wait longer.

rations, was she at last subdued, and fell the Victim of his lawless Flame.

O'erwhelm'd in Tenderness, and lost to every Thought but that of giving Pleasure to the dear Undoer, was she for a time content with what she had done, nor once imagined how despicable she was now grown in his Eyes for that very Action which she had yielded to but to endear him more: while lull'd, by his continued Ardours into a Belief that he was all Sincerity; how tranquil was her State! But when Indifference came, and cold Neglect, how much beyond the reach of dull Description were the Agonies of her distracted Soul! — To enhance the Misery of her Condition, she found herself with Child; with Child by a Man who was already tired with her Embraces, despised her Tenderness, and from whom she had not the least hope of receiving any Reparation[23] for the Shame to which he had reduced her. — Now was she touch'd with a just Sensibility of the Crime she had been guilty of to Heaven, and to herself: — Now did Reflection glare full of Horror on her affrighted View: — Now did the sharpest Stings of late Repentance torture her afflicted Soul, and drive her to Despair.

Concealing, however, as much as possible, how far she had discovered his Ingratitude, she let him know the Consequence of their unlicenced Joys, and press'd him to marry her in Terms so moving and so tender, that had he not been abandoned by all Sense of Honour or of Justice, he would, indeed, have fulfill'd what he so often, and so solemnly had vow'd: But he had now obtained his wanton Purpose, Desire was satiated; and of that stock of Fondness and Admiration which his Breast lately glow'd with, there scarce remained a common Pity for the ruin he had caused. When first she mentioned Marriage to him; he evaded the Question, and seem'd but to *delay*, not absolutely *deny* what she required; but soon he threw aside Hypocrisy, and plainly told her he had other Views: that it was not consistent with his Circumstances to take a Wife without a Portion, and that his Father had before his Death exacted from him a Vow

[23] *Reparation* a hasty marriage to cover up the shame of pregnancy.

never to marry, but where at least an Equality of Fortune afforded him a prospect of future Happiness. Mild, and gentle as
he had ever found *Glicera*, he now perceived her Soul could
change as well as his had done. Never was Rage carried to a
greater height than hers, — she seem'd all Fury — and distracted
with her Wrongs, beholding the cruel Author of them rather
exulting than any way compassionating her Misery, she said
and did a thousand things which could not be reconciled to
Reason: — Impossible is it to describe her Behaviour such as it
was, therefore I shall only say that proportioned to the *Love* she
had born him while she believed him *true*, was her *Resentment*
when she knew him *false*. With an Indifference the most stabbing to a Lover's Soul did he listen to her Upbraidings, and
coolly telling her that if he stay'd much longer, she might be in
danger of railing herself quite out of breath, made a scornful
Bow, and took his Leave.

Some perhaps, into whose hands this little Narrative may
fall, may have shar'd the same Fate with poor *Glicera*; like her
have been betrayed by the undoing Artifices of deluding Men;
like her have been abandoned by the Perfidy of an ungrateful
Lover to Shame, to late Repentance, and never-ending Griefs;
and it is those only, who can conceive what 'twas she suffered,
or know to compassionate the labouring Anguish of a Heart
abus'd and inspir'd in this superlative degree. The happy *Insensible*, or the *untempted* Fair, are little capable of judging her
Distress, and will be apt to say her *Misfortune* was no more than
what her *Folly* merited: yet let those pitiless Deriders of her
Frailty take care to fortify their Minds with *Virtue*, or they will
but vainly depend on the Force of their own Resolution to
defend them from the same Fate she mourn'd.

She now found that she had a greater Stock of Resentment in
her Soul, than, till it was rouz'd by this Treatment, she could
have believed; sooner would she have sent a Dagger to his
Heart, than any way subjected herself to a second Insult, by
inviting him to return, or testifying the least remains of Tenderness, had not the Condition she was in compell'd her to it, and

forced her trembling Hand, in spite of Pride, to write him the following Epistle.

To the Ungrateful and Perfidious
MELLADORE.

ILL-treated, forsaken as I am, and scorned, perhaps the Remonstrances made you by my *Pen* may be more effectual than those of my *Tongue*; yet had you Love or Honour, Gratitude or Pity, they would be needless: To what purpose then, may you say, do I write? — I have indeed, but little hope of Success on a Man of the Disposition I now find you are, and would sooner chuse Death than the Obligation to you on my own account. — But Oh! there is a tender Part of both of us, which claims a Parent's care: That dear Unborn, that guiltless Consequence of our mutual Raptures, starting within me, makes me feel a Mother's Fondness, and a Mother's Duty: — Nature, Religion, Pity, and Love, all plead in its behalf, and bid me leave no Means untry'd to save its helpless Innocence from Shame and Want, and all the Miseries of an unfriending World;[24] — be just then to your Vows — Remember you are mine as much in the Eye of Heaven, as if a thousand Witnesses had confirm'd our Contract: The Ceremony of the Church is but ordained to bind those Pairs, who of themselves want Constancy and Resolution to keep the Promise which Passion forms. — How often have you sworn I was your Wife, that you considered me as no other, nor would relinquish that right my Love had given you over me for all the World calls dear? — But you are altered since, and I too sadly prove your boasted Virtue but Hypocrisy, a Feint to hire me to Destruction. — Ah! how inhuman, how barbarous has been your Usage of me! If with the loss of my expected

[24]*helpless Innocence from. . .unfriending World* Glicera refers to the illegitimacy of her unborn child and the difficulties it would face. Bastard children became the unwanted responsibility of the parish in which they were born and were subject to ill treatment and neglect. Bastards' legal rights were, according to Blackstone, "very few, being only such as [they] can *acquire*, for [they] can *inherit* nothing, being looked upon as the son[s] of nobody, and sometimes called *filius nullius*, sometimes *filius populi*" (Blackstone, Bk. I, chap. 16, 447).

Dower I also lost your Heart, why did you not then reveal it? —
What Provocation had I e'er given you, that you should join
with Fortune to undo me? *join*, did I say? — how infinitely inferior was my Unhappiness in being deprived of Wealth, when
compared to those more valuable Treasures thy fatal Passion
has robb'd me of. — My Innocence, my Reputation, and my
Peace of Mind by thee destroy'd, no more to be retrieved! —
tormenting Thought! Reflection all distracting! ease me of it,
or to the Number of thy monstrous Actions add yet one more,
and kill me; the worst of Deaths, is a mild Fate to what I now
endure, — and will be a kind Cruelty not only to me, but to the
little Wretch I bear: — Let the Sword finish that ruin which
Deceit begun, and send us both from Shame, Reproach, and
never-ending Woe. — Answer this not, till you have well weigh'd
the Circumstances which compel me to write in a manner so
vastly different from what I once believed I ever should have
cause to do, and make me now subscribe my self no other than

Your most injured and

afflicted GLICERA.

This she ordered to be given into no Hand but his own, to the
end that he might not have any pretence to avoid answering it:
but being now wholly taken up with making himself appear as
agreeable as he could in the Eyes of a fine Lady, who was
represented to him as a great Fortune, he either forgot, or had
not leisure to compassionate the Complaints of the undone
Glicera. — For some days did she remain in expectation, but
hearing nothing from him, all the little Remains of Patience
which her Misfortunes had left her being exhausted, she urg'd a
second time the Certainty of her Fate in these Lines.

To the unworthy MELLADORE.

THO' void of Hope, as thou art of all Sense of Honour, Gratitude, or Humanity, I once more dare thee to avow thy
Purpose, — tell me at once what 'tis I must expect: — No longer
seek by silence to skreen thy Perfidy, but boldly own the Fiends
that lurk within thee; — what is there in me to awe thee, when

Heaven has not the power to do it? Scarce is there a possibility that thou art not the vilest and most detestable of thy whole betraying Specie, yet is there something in my Heart which will not suffer me to assure my self thou art so, till thy own Words destroy Suspence, and put it past my power to make a doubt: — Still, therefore shall I persecute thee with Complaints, — still testify the Agonies of my distracted Soul, divided between *Love* and *Rage*: — Continue with alternate *Soothings* and *Revilings*, as either of the opposing Passions rise, to weary and *perplex* each future Moment of him, whose *Happiness* was once my only Care. — Ah! what a dreadful Revolution has thy Ingratitude caused within my Breast — my Thoughts before serene as an unruffled Sea, now toss'd and hurried by tumultuous Passions, o'erwhelm my Reason, and drive me into Madness.[25] — O that as I have heard, I could be certain also, that when supportless Injuries like mine distress the Soul, and drive it from its clayey Mansion, it still has power to wander and disturb the cruel Author of the Wrongs it suffers; how gladly would I welcome Death in hope of Vengeance, in horrid Shapes would I appear to thy affrighted Eyes, distract thy Dreams, and sleeping and waking be ever before thee! — O what a Whirl of wild Ideas possess my troubled Brain — the Tortures of the Damn'd exceed not what I feel; — thou Monster of thy Sex, thou wert not sure of Woman born, thy Mother's Softness must have given some Tincture of Good-nature to thee, but thou art savage all! The Cruelty of Tygers is within thee, and all the base Subtilty of the betraying Crocodile,[26] — Perdition seize thee: How canst thou,

---

[25]*now toss'd and hurried. . .into Madness* The sea storm imagery is reminiscent of Belvidera's mad speech in Thomas Otway's tragedy *Venice Preserv'd* (1682), 5.2, 5.4. The rest of Glicera's letter — her desire to haunt Melladore waking and sleeping after she dies — seems to allude to John Donne's poem "The Apparition" (1633).

[26]*base Subtilty of the betraying Crocodile* the crocodile was fabulously said to weep, to allure people for the purpose of devouring them; hence, a person who weeps or makes a show of sorrow hypocritically or with a malicious purpose (OED) such as Melladore's plot to seduce Glicera.

darest thou use me thus? Heaven will revenge my Wrongs, tho'
it denies the Power to

The Miserable
GLICERA.

Whoever has the least Knowledge of the Temper of Mankind, will believe a Letter of this sort would have but little Effect
on the Person to whom it was sent. Instead of compassionating
her Misfortunes, he took the Opportunity she gave him of reproaching him to come to a down-right Quarrel; and having
taken a little time for Consideration, answer'd her in these
Terms.

To GLICERA.

I Know not to what end you give yourself and me these needless
Troubles: I thought you Mistress of a better Understanding
than to imagine an Amour of the nature our's was, should last
for ever: — 'Tis not in Reason, 'tis not in Nature to retain per-
petual Ardours for the same Object. — The very word *Desire*
implies an Impossibility of continuing after the Enjoyment of
that which first caused its being: — Those Longings, those Im-
patiences so pleasing to your Sex, cannot but be lost in Possession, for who can wish for what he has already? — Marriage, as
you justly observe, obliges the Pair once united by those Tyes to
wear a *Show* of Love; but where is the Man who has one Month
become a Husband, that can with truth aver he feels the same
unbated Fondness for his Wife, as when her untasted Charms
first won him to her Arms. — Had Circumstances concur'd, I
could, however, have been content to drag those Chains with
you, so uneasy to be borne, by most of those who wear them;
but since Affairs have happened contrary to both our Expectations, lay the fault on Fate, and not on me, who would else have
still avow'd my self to be what I once was,

Your most Affectionate
MELLADORE.

P.S. I would have you take notice that this is an Answer to the
first of your Epistles; — the other I think not worthy of a serious

Regard, and would advise you to send no more to me on any score, this being the last you will receive from me. And am still so much your Friend as to wish your Peace; which, if you really love me with that Ardour you pretend, you can never retrieve, till you resolve to think no more of what has past between us: there being a Necessity that we must part for ever.

It must be something more terrible than Storms or Whirlwinds, or the Roar of foaming Seas, which can describe the Hurricane of her outrageous Soul at reading this Letter: — Reason she had none, nor Reflection, but what served to bring a thousand direful Ideas of approaching Misery before her Eyes; — more than once did she in the first Gust of her Passion endeavour to lay violent Hands on her own Life, but was prevented by a Servant Maid, in whose presence she received these stabbing Lines. The unusual Force of those Emotions with which she was agitated, threw her into a Mother's Pangs long before the time prefix'd by Nature, her Delivery was arriv'd, and by that means the Consequence of her too easy Love proved no more than an Abortion. — The Danger to which this Accident expos'd her, made her Life despair'd of by every body about her; and in spite of the late Attempts she had made on herself, she no sooner found she was given over by the Skilful, than she verified that Saying of the Poets:

> — *The Thoughts of Death*
> *To one near Death are dreadful.*[27]

Tho' press'd with Ills, which neither Philosophy nor Religion can enable us to sustain with Patience, and every Hour we wish to be no more, we fear to pass the Gates of Life, and travel that dark and unknown Road whence none return to tell what they

---

[27] *The Thoughts of Death*
   To one near Death are dreadful.
This quotation has not been identified. Haywood often quotes many Restoration playwrights, having been an actress herself, and may not remember the source of all of her quotations.

have met[.] 'Tis in general so with us: — Some, indeed, may have a greater share of Fortitude than poor *Glicera*, but few there are who hear unmov'd the Warnings of their Fate, especially in Youth.

The extreme Fear she had of Death, in some measure contributed to prolong her Life; for all her Cares being buried in that superior one, the Distraction of her Mind abated: — To this may be also another Reason added, which was, that her desire of Living made her readily comply with every thing prescribed her by the Physicians; and their Skill and Care, join'd to her own strength of Nature, at last restor'd her to that Health, which none who saw her in her Illness imagined she ever would have enjoy'd again.

But while she languished in Pangs which were look'd on as the Harbingers of Death, was the perfidious *Melladore* triumphing in a Bridegroom's Joys. He was married to a young Maid call'd *Helena*, whose Father being lately dead, was reputed to be worth 5000 Crowns,[28] and those were Charms which in his avaritious Eyes far exceeded those *Glicera* was possess'd of, and tho' infinitely inferior to her in every Perfection both of Mind and Body, was thought worthy his most tender Devoirs,[29] while the other unpitied, unregarded, was almost dying under the Miseries which he alone had brought upon her.

When she was told this last Proof of his remorseless Infidelity, the News was near throwing her into a Condition almost as dangerous as that which she had lately escap'd; her Passions, however, being much weaken'd by the decay of her bodily Strength, she fell not into those Ravings, which drove her almost to Madness at the first Causes she had to think him false: And in a few Months she not only regain'd her Health, but also a greater Tranquility of Mind than could be expected in a Condition such as her's. — The Memory of her Wrongs, however, left her not a Moment, and by degrees settled so implaca-

[28] *5000 Crowns* £1250 (or approximately $75,000 modern); an impressive dowry.

[29] *Devoirs* dutiful respects, courteous attentions, addresses (OED).

ble a hatred in her Nature, not only to *Melladore*, but to that whole undoing Sex, that she never rejoic'd so much as when she heard of the Misfortunes of any of them.

The Affair between her and *Melladore* being blaz'd abroad, was of too much Disadvantage to her Reputation, to suffer her to imagine she should be able to make her Fortune by Marriage, tho' several there were that addressed her in Terms which had the appearance of Honourable; but she had already experienced Mankind, and was not to be deceived again by the most specious Pretences: despising therefore the whole Sex, she resolved to behave to them in a manner which might advance both her Interest and Revenge; and as nothing is capable of giving more Vexation to a Lover, than a Disappointment when he thinks himself secure from the Fears of it, she gave Encouragement to the Hopes of as many as sollicited her. — She received their Treats and Presents, smil'd on all, tho' never so Old or Disagreeable; nor indeed was it a greater Task, to feign a Tenderness for the most *Ugly* than the *Loveliest* of Mankind — for all alike were hateful to her Thoughts.

Among the Number of those whom her Beauty attracted, and the hope of gaining her more firmly engaged, was an *Alderman*, immensely Rich, but so Old that none who had beheld his wither'd Face, and shaking Limbs, would have believed that in those shrivell'd Veins there was a Warmth sufficient to maintain *Life*, much less to propagate *Desire*. His palsied Tongue, and toothless Gums, however, mumbled out a strange Fervency of Passion;[30] and tho' it was scarce possible to refrain laughing in his Face, yet did she listen to him with a Seriousness which made him not doubt but that he should be in time as happy as he could wish. His Age and Dotage making her believe she should be able to profit herself more by him than any other of her Enamorato's, induced her to treat him with a double Portion of seeming Kindness, nor did he fail to return the Favours

---

[30]*Alderman*.. The Alderman's description is reminiscent of the elderly and sexually perverted Senator Antonio and his relationship with the courtezan, Aquilina, in Otway's *Venice Preserv'd* (1682). See 2.1, and 3.1.

she was pleased to grace him with; scarce ever did he visit her without testifying his Gratitude for the deference she paid him in some fine Present. — She abounded in Rings, Toys for her Watch,[31] Plate of all kinds,[32] and Jewels; but all these were no more than so many Earnests of his future Zeal: — The last and greatest Favour was yet to come, and he assured her that there wanted only that to engage him to make her a Settlement,[33] which should support her in a manner as grand, as that in which the Wife of *Melladore* at present liv'd. But vastly different were the Designs which made her treat him in the sort she did, from those which he imagined them to be; and resolving to make the most of his Folly, she let into the Secret of her Thoughts a young Woman with whom she was exceeding intimate, called *Laphelia*. This Confidante, who had a ready Wit, to try the Force of this old Wretch's Love, was left sometimes to entertain him, while *Glicera* pretended to be engaged elsewhere on some extraordinary Business. And when he would be talking of her, and almost exhausting the little stock of Breath left him in Encomiums on the Beauty of his absent Mistress, in this fashion would the other reply to him: *Grubguard*,[34] said she, (for that was the Name of this decrepid Lover,) I wonder not that you should be charm'd with *Glicera*, who is without exception the loveliest Woman in the World, but I am amaz'd that a Man of your Sense should go so wrong a way to work for your Designs: — Do you believe that she will ever be brought to like that formal Dress and Behaviour with which you accost her? — She that has a thousand young Noblemen dying at her Feet,

---

[31] *Toys for her Watch* small ornaments or curiosities to hang from a watch chain. "Toy" is applied to things of diminuitive size, flimsy construction, or petty character, as if intended for sport or diversion rather than serious use (OED).

[32] *Plate of all kinds* silver coins, utensils or ornaments (OED).

[33] *make her a Settlement* to establish her in life, in marriage, in an office or employment; the act or process of regulating or putting on a permanent footing; the act of establishing (public affairs, etc.) in security or tranquility. In law: the act of settling property upon a person (OED).

[34] *Grubguard* grub (noun): a short, dwarfish fellow; a money-grubber. (verb): to search in an undignified, abject, or grovelling manner; to rummage (OED).

each in the Habit of an *Adonis*.[35] Embroidery, Powder, and
Perfume are infinitely taking to our Sex. — A very Angel of a
Man with a Bob wig,[36] a Hat uncock'd and flapping o'er his
Eyes like *Obadiah* in the Play,[37] no Sword, and a dirty Pair of
Gloves, would be detestable in a Woman's Eyes. Humph, *reply'd
the Dotard*, (after a little Pause) I took *Glicera* for a Person of
more Understanding than to prefer an outward Finery to the
intrinsick Virtues of her Lover. — My Passion for her is violent
and strong, 'tis sincere without Dissimulation or Hypocrisy; —
then for my Constancy, no Martyr would suffer more for fair
Glicera than would her faithful *Grubguard*. — But if 'tis Dress must
please her, I can afford to wear as fine Clothes as any Man,
and, it may be, become them as well. Scarce could *Laphelia*
contain her self from bursting into a loud Laughter at these
Words; but she forbore till after he was gone, and relating the
Discourse which had pass'd between them to *Glicera*, nothing
could afford greater Diversion to them both, unless it were the
sight of him the next Visit he made, wholly transform'd from
what he had been. — Never was an Object of more Ridicule,
and tho' they had form'd a most comical Idea in their Minds of
what he would appear; for *Laphelia* was certain he would endeavour to ingratiate himself by this means, yet it was infinitely
short of the Reality. — A white Perriwig with a huge Fore-top,
Clothes trim'd with Silver, a long Sword with a brocaded Rib-
band hanging to it, and every Implement of the most perfect
Beau, which, join'd to a diminutive Stature, small Face and
Limbs, made him look exactly like one of those little Imitators

[35]*Adonis* In Greek mythology, a youth beloved by Venus for his beauty;
hence, ironically, a beau or dandy (OED).

[36]*Bob wig* The long bob covered the neck; the short exposed it. Both had a
centre parting until the 1730s. The hair framed the face and ended in a roll curl
or bushy wave round the back of the neck (Cunnington, 91).

[37]*Obadiah in the Play* the pompous, Puritan clerk who is made drunk by the
Irish servant, Teague, in Sir Robert Howard's 1662 comedy, *The Committee*.
Another example of Haywood's frequent allusions to the stage.

of Humanity,[38] which are carried about Streets to make Sport for Children.

Nor was his Habit the greatest part of the Jest, his whole Deportment was also chang'd; the *Minuit* and *Boree*[39] Steps which he had learn'd about some sixty or seventy Years past, he now recalled to mind, and would now and then attempt to cut a Caper as he walk'd cross the Room, to present his Snuff-box to the Ladies, cramb'd full of *Orangerée*:[40] — But in the midst of these fine Airs, Age unluckily expos'd itself, and down he fell at the Feet of his Mistress, more through Weakness than Excess of Passion. — This Accident, in spite of all they had resolv'd, made them burst into an immoderate Laughter, which had like to have spoil'd all; for the *Alderman*, too conscious of the just Cause he had given them for Mirth, was a little out of humour at it, and began to make an aukward Excuse, that having been at a Country-Dancing some time before, he had sprain'd his Ancle, which had ever since been weak. *Glicera*, vex'd that she had so far discovered the contemptible Opinion she had of him, had her Face immediately cover'd with a Scarlet-blush; but having a vast deal of ready Wit, recovering herself from the Confusion she had been in, I beg a thousand Pardons, *said she*, for the Ill-manners I have doubtless seem'd guilty of by so untimely a Mirth: but I assure you, *Sir!* it was wholly my own Folly I was ridiculing; for having a desire that my Apartment should be particularly Nice to-day, I made my Maid scour the Floor with new Milk, and the Cream has occasion'd so great a Slipperiness in the Boards, that I have twice myself had the same Misfortune which has befallen you. She was just telling me the Story when

---

[38]*little Imitators of Humanity* a monkey. It was fashionable during the 18th century to have monkeys as pets (see *Spectator* no. 343) and outfit them as little men. Haywood again emphasizes Grubguard's physical littleness and his low nature.

[39]*Minuit and Boree* Minuet: a slow stately dance in triple measure, for two dancers. Boree: a French, rustic dance (OED). Once again, Haywood empha-sizes Grubguard's decrepit age, and his inability to please physically the young Glicera.

[40]*Orangerée* snuff scented with orange-flower extract (OED).

you came in, *added Laphelia*, willing to second what she had said,
and if my Mirth must have been fatal to me, I could not for my
Soul have forborn it, to see the ill Success of my Friend's over-
great Care to please. This Excuse passing for a current one, the
transmografied Lover[41] resum'd his good Humour, and continued his Grimaces and affected Manner of Behaviour to so ex-
travagant a degree, that more than once the Ladies were in
danger of relapsing into that Error which had lately cost their
Invention some pains to extricate themselves from.

Laphelia, to carry on the Jest, did not fail however, the next
time she had an Opportunity, to tell him that her fair Friend
was wonderfully pleased with the Change she observ'd in him,
and that she did not doubt but he would find the good Effects
of it in a short time: But they having contrived together, how
they might make a better Advantage of this Infatuation than
meerly Sport; she told him that as he had begun, he must also
perfect himself in all the Accomplishments of the other End of
the Town; he must carry them to the Play, the Opera, and
Masquerades, and after attending them Home, must sit down
to Gaming. No Man ever gain'd his will on a fine Lady, *said
she*, till he had first lost a good Sum to her at Cards; — nothing
discovers the Passion of a Lover so much as parting freely with
his Money, and there is no other way of doing it
handsomely: — Besides, *continued she*, play will give you a thousand Opportunities of expressing your Love and Gallantry: —
You forget what you are doing, throw down one Card instead
of another, commit a thousand Errors in the Game, and all
through excess of Passion; — you can think of nothing in the
presence of your Mistress but herself: — In fine, there are so
many pretty little Airs a Man may give himself this way, that
'tis impossible he should not be agreeable. *Grubguard* listened
with a wonderful Attention to this Discourse, and having met
with so encouraging a Reception from *Glicera*, that he had not
doubted obtaining the last Favour; yet finding she still evaded

---

[41] *transmografied Lover* altered in appearance; utterly, grotesquely or strangely
transformed (OED).

the grant of it, he imagin'd indeed that there was something more she expected from him: He was not unacquainted with the loss of her Fortune, and her Sufferings on account of *Melladore*, and knew very well that she must want Money; it therefore seemed feasible to him that she had made *Laphelia*, who he knew was dearly beloved by her, to talk to him in this manner. Resolving therefore to comply with the Humour, he thank'd her for the Advice she had given him, and told her he would most certainly obey it.

Nor did he do any otherwise than he had said, there was not the least particular of the Injunction laid upon him that he did not observe, with all the Exactness imaginable; and the Sums which every Night he lost to *Glicera*, took from her in a very few Weeks all need of lamenting her want of Money. — In this manner did she continue to delude him for a considerable Time: a true *Lover* like a *Camelion* can subsist for a long while on Air,[42] and stedfastly believing that the Measures he took would certainly put him in possession of his Wishes in the end, he waited with Patience for the happy Minute.

But it was not on this old Dotard alone that *Glicera* had Power, a great Number of much younger and wittier Men gave her the Opportunity of revenging on that Sex the Injuries she had received from one of them; and having as large a Share of Sense as Beauty, knew so well how to manage the Conquests she gain'd, that not one whose *Heart* confess'd the Triumph of her Eyes, but made a Sacrifice also of his *Purse*. — So magnificent was she in the Trophies of her Slave, that few Court-*Beauties* appeared more ornamented then did this *City*-Belle, when ever she appeared in any publick Place; and never did a Woman passionately in love take greater Pains to captivate the ador'd Object of her Affections than did this fair *Jilt*,[43] to appear amia-

---

[42] *a Camelion. . .on Air* chameleons, from their inanimate appearance and power of existing for long periods without food, were supposed to live on air (OED).

[43] *fair Jilt* "a woman who gives her lover hopes, and deceives him" (Johnson); one who capriciously casts off a lover after giving him encouragement (OED).

ble in the Eyes of Mankind. Tho' she had enough overcome all
Thoughts of *Melladore*, not to languish for his Return, or even
wish to see him; yet the Hatred which his Ingratitude had
created in her Mind was so fix'd and rooted there, that it became part of her Nature, and she seem'd born only to give
Torment to the whole Race of Man, nor did she know another
Joy in Life. In this Position let us leave her for a while, each
Day attracting to her worshipp'd Shrine some new Adorer, gay,
pleas'd and vain in conquering Beauty and superior Charms,
and see what Fate in the mean time attended the perfidious
Melladore, whose cruel Treatment had first occasioned so strange
a Change in her once gentle and unartful Soul.

In some few days after his Marriage with *Helena*, he went to
receive her Fortune; but how terribly Just was his Disappointment, when the Banker in whose hands it was lodg'd, told him,
that the Moment before he came he had receiv'd a *Caveat* to put
a stop to his Payment of the whole or any part of it, till a
material Question should be decided between the Lawyers:
Which was, that the next of Kin to the Father of *Helena*, ob-
jected that the Marriage Ceremony between that Gentleman
and her Mother had never been perform'd, and dar'd the old
Lady, who was still living, to the Proof. Full of the extremest
Vexation did *Melladore* return home with this News; but *Helena*,
who at the hearing it was not much less perplex'd, immediately
sending for her Mother, they both grew more satisfied on her
protesting that it was only a malicious Prosecution, and that
nothing could be more easy than it was for her to prove her
Marriage.

Now were the best Lawyers consulted, and the Suit on both
sides carryed on with the utmost Vigour, the Gentlemen of the
long Robe flattering their Clients of each Party with hopes of
Success: The truth is, both made out their several Cases in so
fair a manner, and had so great a Number of Evidences ready to
attest the Truth of what they said, that they deceived themselves; which makes good the Proverb, that says, whoever con-
ceals the truth of his *Distemper* from his *Physician*, or the *Cause* he

would defend from his *Lawyer*, is sure of being worsted.[44] Melladore relying on the Assurances made him by his Mother-in-law,
talk'd of nothing but the Damages he should recover of his
Adversaries, and spent his Money freely in Treats and Fees for
extraordinary Diligence, not doubting but that all would be
returned to him with ample Interest. Thus did he exult till the
Day appointed for the Tryal on the Examination of Witnesses:
Those who appear'd for the Mother of *Helena*, appear'd so distracted in their Evidences, contradicted each other, and committed so many Errors, that the Judge had good reason to
believe they had been corrupted; therefore ordering them to be
put apart, he questioned them one by one, on which they were
easily detected of Perjury, and *Melladore*, *Helena*, and her
Mother hiss'd out of Court with the utmost Derision; the whole
Effects of the Deceas'd decreed to the young Gentleman who
began the Process, and *Melladore*, for so ill defending it, condemn'd to pay the Expence.

What was now the Condition of this guilty and unhappy
Man? He had now not only married a Wife without a Fortune,
but also a Woman basely born, and in whose Disposition he had
reason to believe there was some tincture of her Mother's Nature: Besides all this, the prodigious Charge he had been at, in
carrying on the Law, had very much broke in upon his Stock,
he was not only oblig'd to call in several Sums he had out at
Interest, but was likewise compell'd to borrow: Yet did not the
Pride and Extravagance of *Helena* abate, by these Mortifica-
tions; she would keep as many Servants as before, as good a
Table, and wear as rich Clothes: this occasion'd many bitter
Quarrels between them, which in a very little time intirely
eras'd all the former Tenderness that either had for the other.
He endeavour'd to exert the Authority of a Husband in re-
straining her Expences; she show'd herself a very Wife in the
worst Sense, and without any Consideration of the ill Circum-

---

[44]*Proverb. . .worsted* A proverb popular from 1573 ("Conceale not the truthe
from the Physition and Lawyer"). Haywood seems to have added the explicit
moral tag, "is sure of being worsted" (Tilley, P261: 535).

stances to which they were in danger of being reduc'd by her riotous manner of Life, had no bounds to her Desires, but sought the immediate Gratification of them, let it cost what it would: And to what Extremes sometimes her Inclinations were capable of transporting her, he discover'd soon after the loss of the Law-Suit.

Happening to come into her Chamber on a sudden, he surpriz'd her with a Paper in her Hand, on which her Eyes being intently fix'd, she saw him not till he was very near her; but as soon as she perceiv'd him, she attempted to put it in her Pocket. The Confusion which overspread her Face as she was about to do so, excited his Curiosity, and made him not doubt but that there was something extraordinary in it; he therefore demanded to see it, which she refusing, he went to seize by Force: they struggled for some time, but his Strength at last prevailing, he took it from her; and as if his Misfortunes were not already great enough, he found an Addition to them in the following Lines.

To the Lovely H E L E N A.

BAD as you believe your Husband's Circumstances, I can assure you they are infinitely worse than you imagine; his ready Money is not only gone, but he is about to mortgage those Acres which were design'd your Jointure,[45] in case Fortune had been as kind to you as your Virtues merited. I heard this account of him last Night from one perfectly acquainted with his Affairs: — I would, therefore, once more endeavour to persuade you, to save what you can out of that general Ruin in which you else will certainly, and shortly be involv'd. — The Ship I told you of, sets sail for *Holland* in a few days; pack up your Jewels, and what other valuable Things you have, with all possible expedition, and leave this unworthy Husband. — I have provided a

---

[45] *Jointure* "an annuity for the widow for the rest of her days" (Stone, 15); the amount of money or property, decided upon by the groom's father, to be given to the bride in the event of her widowhood. In his letter, Villagnon hopes that Melladore will die and leave Helena available and in possession of his land.

Concealment for you till the departure of the Vessel begins the happy Æra of our Lives, and begins our Voyage to a Land where we may live, and love, uninterrupted by any jealous Eyes: — Let your Answer be left for me at the usual Place, if you cannot come abroad. — Farewell my Angel, — I long to feast on those luxurious Joys you have yet but permitted me to taste, and to prove the eternal Vigour of

My adorable Helena's

most devoted Slave,

VILLAGNAN.

This *Villagnan* was a kind of a Merchant,[46] one at least who by retailing some petty Commodities between *England* and *Holland*, assumed to himself that Name. *Melladore* knew him well, he had frequently bought such Goods of him as he dealt in, and it was by that means he had an Opportunity of conversing with *Helena*, and discovering enough of her Disposition to encourage him to make a Declaration of Love to her. But never was Surprize or Rage equal to the Force of both these Passions in the Soul of *Melladore* at reading this Letter; little could he have believ'd, without so convincing a Proof, that such a Man would have attempted the Honour of a Woman like *Helena*, much less that her Pride would have suffer'd her to have rewarded his Love, or even condescended to listen to any Discourses on that Subject from one so infinitely inferior to her in every Circumstance. He having never felt much more for her than an Indifference, which by his late Uneasiness on her account was grown into a kind of a distaste, now turn'd to a perfect loathing on the knowledge of her Falshood: — He upbraided her in terms which let her see there was not the least remains of Tenderness for her in his Heart; — if there had, *Grief* would have been mingled with his *Indignation*, and his *Sorrow* at the discovery that he had a Rival in her Love, been equal to the *Rage* which the Injury she had done his

---

[46]*a kind of Merchant* a smuggler, probably of contraband Flanders lace and/or Holland linen into England.

and her own Honour caused. But instead of that tender Concern which a truly affectionate Husband could not have avoided testifying even in the midst of his Reproaches; all his Looks and Words denoted only Hate, inveterate Hate, and the most keen Disdain. She, on the other side, made show of as little Regret, neither denying, nor excusing the Crime she had been guilty of, but behaving with a haughty Sullenness: All the Answer he could be able to get from her, being only that the Usage she had of late received from him was sufficient to provoke any Woman. He so little endur'd her in his sight, that he was some time in debate with himself whether he should by confining her take care to prevent her from dishonouring him for the future; or by leaving her to her Liberty, suffer her to take the advice of her *Enamorato*, and by that means get rid of her. He now repented he had seen the Letter, which if he had not, she had infallibly been gone; but now to endure her leaving him in this manner, he thought would look too tame, and subject him to the ridicule of the World; not for any Love of her Society, therefore, but for the sake of his own Character, did he disappoint her Lover's Hopes, by locking her into a Garret, of which, suffering none but himself to keep the Key, nor to go in to carry her Food to sustain Life; he took from her all possibility of escaping, till he heard the Ship mention'd in the Letter had put out to Sea, and in it the Man so charming in *Helena*'s Eyes. Then did he with an Air wholly compos'd of Scorn set open the Doors, and tell her she was free to go to her dear *Villagnan* if she could find the way to him; tho' he had taken care she should carry no more out of his House than she brought into it, having secur'd what Jewels and Plate he had presented her with before and since she was his Wife, leaving at her disposal only a few Clothes, and not the best even of those.

But in this Kingdom how great is the Privilege of Wives! how dangerous is it for a Husband to irritate them, tho' on the most justifiable Provocation! and generally speaking, the most guilty, are the least able to endure Reproof, as a celebrated Poet justly observes;

Forgiveness to the Injur'd does belong,
But they ne'er pardon who have done
the wrong.[47]

The Severity with which *Helena* found herself treated by *Melladore*, notwithstanding the Cause she had given him, rouz'd all that was vindictive in her Nature, and regarding him with equal Hate, meditated nothing but how she should be able to return the Indignities with which he us'd her: Nor was it long before she found the Means. She went to the House of a Woman who had been the Confidante of her Amour with *Villagnan*, and was a Person perfectly skill'd in all the little Artifices of the Town. By her advice she took up, on the Credit of her Husband,[48] not only all manner of Apparel, Jewels, Plate, rich Furniture, but also several large Sums of Money; *Melladore* retaining yet the Reputation of being able to discharge much greater Debts.

The Noise, however, of her being separated from her Husband, made every one bring in their Bills much sooner than otherwise they would have done; and 'tis hard to say, whether Astonishment, or Rage, was the most predominant over the Soul of this unhappy Husband when he found what she had done. He could not have imagin'd, that considering the Disadvantages she already lay under in every Circumstance, she would have dared to have acted in this manner; but so he found it, to compleat his Ruin: nor was there any Possibility of evading the Payment of those Persons who had given her Credit. How truly wretched now had a few Months made the once prosperous, rich, gay, haughty *Melladore*; and how severely did the unerring Hand of Providence revenge the Injuries he had done *Glicera!* Scarce could one think there was a Woe in store superior to those already named; yet did he hereafter meet with

---

[47] *Forgiveness to the Injur'd does belong,*

But they ne'er pardon who have done the wrong.   unidentified quotation.

[48] *Credit of her Husband* A husband was liable for all debts incurred by his wife. Thus, an abandoned wife, like Helena, "could spend money for necessaries appropriate to her station in life, and then urge a creditor to sue her . . . husband for the debt" (Stone, 15).

one, which when compar'd, all others seem'd light and insignificant.

The vast Expences which had attended the Law-Suit, the riotous Manner in which he liv'd after his Marriage with *Helena*, her Extravagancies at that time, and her Contrivances since her Elopement of undoing him, reduc'd him to mortgage the last Stake he now had left him; and so closely did avenging Fate pursue him, that as if it was not a sufficient Punishment for the Crime he had been guilty of, in breach of Vows, that he had met with those very Misfortunes in the Woman he made choice of, which to avoid, he had made himself that Criminal; he must also have the Person he had wrong'd, the Arbitratress of his Destiny, and become wholly in the power of one from whom he neither could, nor ought to hope for Mercy.

So was it order'd by the divine Dispensation, to render his Shame the greater, that Alderman *Grubguard* was the Person to whom he mortgaged his Lands. Had he known the Attachments he was under to *Glicera*, or indeed that he had been of her Acquaintance, sooner would he have leap'd a Precipice, plung'd himself into outrageous Seas, done any thing rather than have suffer'd his Misfortunes to be known by one, who, in all probability would reveal them to her: But wholly ignorant of the Correspondence held between them, Fate it was that directed him to *Grubguard*, who no sooner had the Mortgage in his hands, than he came to *Glicera*, and rejoiced that he had News to tell her, in which he was very certain she would take delight. He immediately related to her the whole Story: She had before been inform'd of the Disappointment he had met with in his Wife's Affairs, the Law-Suit, how she had been prov'd in open Court Illegitimate, and her Elopement since; but now to be assur'd that he was also ruin'd in his own Fortune, inevitably undone, fill'd her with a Satisfaction so exquisite, that for a moment she thought it impossible it could be exceeded; but soon it gave way to an impatient Desire, which gave her an adequate Share of Disquiet. — She long'd to be the Mistress of that Writing which gave the Person who had it in possession, the Power of all that *Melladore* was now worth in the World, and the little probability there was that *Grubguard* would have Gallantry enough to make a Present of so much consequence, and what had cost him so great a Sum of Money, spread through all her Soul so mortal a Bitter, that it empoison'd all the Sweets her Revenge had tasted at the first News of *Melladore's* Misfortunes. She appear'd in so ill a Humour all the time the *Alderman* stay'd with her, that he imagin'd she still loved that false Man, and that her melancholy proceeded from the Knowledge of his Ruin. This gave our old Enamorato as much Anxiety of Mind as he had Delicacy enough to be capable of; and he long'd for an Opportunity of communicating his Opinion to *Laphelia*, who he fancied was a very great Friend to him, since she had given him advice to new-model his Dress and Behaviour.

Glicera was no less impatient to consult with that Confidante, and as soon as the Departure of the *Alderman* gave her liberty, she sent for her, and acquainted her with what he had related to her concerning *Melladore*, and the Uneasiness she was in to have the Mortgage of his Estate in her possession. *Laphelia* could not forbear chiding her for the exorbitancy of her Wishes: — I never heard of any thing so unreasonable in my Life, *said she*: is it not enough for your Revenge that the Man who has wrong'd you is undone in every Circumstance, without triumphing yourself in the ruin of his Fortune: — That Fortune, answer'd the other, ought to have been mine, had *Melladore* been just, — nor do I think it sufficient that he has lost it, without I also have gain'd it. How often has he sworn, that were he master of ten thousand Worlds, they all were mine: — With what a seeming Zeal and Sanctity, has he invok'd each Saint in Heaven a Witness of his Vows to me! — O never, never can the Breach of them be pardon'd, nor never shall I think my Wrongs repair'd, till I am in possession of my Right; — I mean, *continu'd she*, the *Estate* of *Melladore*; for his *Person*, were he in a Condition, is now become unworthy my Acceptance. *Laphelia* perceiving she was resolute, offer'd no more in contradiction to what she said, but told her that she thought there was little cause for her Uneasiness on the score she had named, for that she durst swear the *Alderman* had Love enough to give her the half of all he was worth, much less would he deny to make her a Present of this Mortgage. O my dear *Laphelia, cry'd she*, could we but bring that about, how happy should I be! Never doubt it, *Glicera, reply'd the other*, leave it to my Management; and as I have begun to instruct him in the Rudiments of Gallantry, depend upon it I will make him perfectly accomplish'd for our Purpose before I have done with him. A vast deal of further Discourse, much to the same purpose, past between them; at the Conclusion of which, it was agreed that *Grubguard* should be invited the next day to play at *Ombre*,[49] with them, and that *Glicera* should be call'd out of the Room, on some pretence that her assisting Friend might have an Opportunity of trying her Wit, and the power she had of deceiving handsomely; after which, Night being pretty well advanc'd, they took leave of each other, the one departed to perfect the Stratagem which as yet was but an Embrio in her inventive Brain, and our fair *Jilt* to pray to all the Powers of Eloquence to assist her in her Designs.

Our old Beau, who had past the Night in Perplexities, equal with those *Glicera* sustain'd, was infinitely pleas'd at the Invitation made him next day, especially when he heard that *Laphelia* was to be there, not doubting but that he should be able to persuade her to let him into the secret of his Mistress's Chagrin; he therefore prevented the appointed Hour,[50] in hope of getting some Opportunity of speaking to her alone: his Impatience, therefore, forwarding the Gratification of the other, soon after he came in, a Servant belonging to the House where *Glicera* lodg'd, told her there was one desir'd to speak with her. On

---

[49]*Ombre* a card-game played by three persons, with forty cards, the eights, nines, and tens of the ordinary pack being thrown out. Popular in the 17th and 18th centuries (OED). Most famous for its appearance in Canto III of Pope's "The Rape of the Lock" (1714). It is significant that Glicera, like Pope's Belinda, plays Ombre (Spanish for "man") with a would-be lover. Both women seem to enjoy the power struggle of the game, and Glicera, especially, becomes more masculine against the effeminate Grubguard.

[50]*prevented the appointed Hour* came before the set time; arrived earlier than the time agreed upon (OED).

which, after having made a short Apology for her absence, she went out of the Room, and left them together.

She was no sooner gone, than *Grubguard* unwilling to lose a Moment, drew his Chair near to that *Laphelia* was sitting in, and began to relate to her the Troubles of his Mind; but she no sooner heard what had occasion'd them, than to save him the labour of further Speech, she interrupted him in this manner: How ingeniously, *said she laughing*, does Love torment his Votaries! — The wanton God prides himself in your Pains, and finds out a thousand Ways to make you delay the Bliss for which you languish; — you are at this time the happiest Man in the World, and do not know it. — Fortune has put in your power the only Means to gain *Glicera's* Favour; and I am certain should the greatest Monarch on Earth become your Rival, he must sue in vain, unless possess'd of one thing, which none but *Grubguard* has the means of bestowing. You speak in Riddles, *Madam!* answer'd the old Dotard, but if there be a possibility of my being happy, why will you not let me know? — There is nothing I would not do to express my Love for Fair *Glicera*, nor to testify my Gratitude to you. I have told her so, *resum'd the artful* Laphelia, I am certain you that have given her so many Proofs of your unbounded Passion, would not scruple to add one more, especially when it will be the last that will be expected from you, and infallibly put you in immediate possession of your Wishes. Ah! *cry'd he*, (in a Transport which was pretty near depriving him of the small Stock of Breath which Nature had left him, to keep the almost expiring Lamp of Life awake;) dear, dear, *Laphelia!* inform me what it is, that I may fly to make this acceptable Offering at the Shrine of my ador'd Goddess, and I will worship thee for the kind Direction. How just was my Opinion of you, *said she*, and how much has *Glicera* wrong'd your wondrous Passion, to imagine you would think such a Trifle too great a Price for the purchase of her Love. Ah the Cruel! (mumbled he out, with his toothless Gums,) but when I get her once in my Possession, I will so revenge myself for all her Coyness. — But sweet Girl, *continued he*, let me know what it is she expects or desires of me, before she resigns me her Paradise of Beauty.

94

Nothing, *reply'd she*, (who now thought he was sufficiently work'd up) but to make her a Present of that Mortgage you received yesterday from *Melladore*. — Here she stop'd, observing all the time his Countenance, in which she saw immediately so great a Change, as made her more than half afraid she had taken all this pains to no purpose; and perceiving he continued in a profound Silence, Heavens! *resum'd she*, has my Penetration deceiv'd me then! — do you hesitate if you should accept so great a Blessing as *Glicera*, when offer'd you on Terms so easy? — Is such a Sum to be valued in competition with the Enjoyment of so fine a Woman? — You quite mistake my Thoughts, *answer'd he*, 'tis not the Money I boggle at; were it twice as much, I could afford to make a Sacrifice of it for my Pleasure: — But alack! I have no Notion, that after all this, I shall be a jot the nearer to the Gratification of my Wishes: — To be plain, I am afraid she has still a kindness for that Spendthrift, and aims to get the Writings out of my hands only to return them into his; — I should then, indeed, be finely fool'd. — O fye, Mr. *Alderman!* I am asham'd of your distrust, *cry'd she*, interrupting him; can you suspect her of so much Folly, or me of such an unexampled piece of Baseness, to persuade you to this Generosity, if I did not know you would find your account in it? — I assure you she hates *Melladore*, and so far from giving him up his Bond, she wishes to have it in her possession, for no other reason than to prosecute the Penalty of it with more Rigour than perhaps any other Person would do. — This I can aver to you is Truth, and durst pawn my Life on the Certainty of what I say: — But, *pursu'd she*, affecting to seem displeas'd, I shall trouble myself no farther between you, — 'tis in vain to endeavour to make People happy, who are resolv'd to be the contrary: — I am only sorry I should say so much in your behalf last Night, since I find *Glicera* was in the right to believe you did not love her half so well as you pretended. She cannot be more belov'd than she is by me, *resum'd the Dotard*, and I have spar'd no Expence either of Time or Money to convince her of it; — but as I know *Melladore* was once very dear to her, you cannot blame my Jealousy; — they say, old Love can never be forgot, and if she should lay this

Stratagem to deliver him his Writings, my easy Nature would be the Jest of the whole Town. Not more than her's, good *Grubguard*, *reply'd* Laphelia, the Injuries she has received from *Melladore* are not of a nature to be pardoned, much less rewarded to the prejudice of another, as this would be to you. — Believe me, I am perfectly acquainted with her very Soul, and know that she has only the extremest Detestation for that unworthy Man; and if you require it, will give you my solemn Oath. — No, no, it needs not, *interrupted he*, let her put me in possession of her Charms, and I will put her in possession of the *Writing*; — this she will not scruple, if she really designs to make me happy. Bless me! *cry'd Laphelia*, with an air of Surprize, I would not have her hear you for the World; — are you mad? — For shame, *Alderman*, recant what you have said. — I wonder how you could forget yourself and her so far, as to be guilty of such a Thought: — you talk as if you were in *Change Alley*,[51] where they chaffer[52] one *Transfer* for another. — Is such a Woman as *Glicera* to be had by way of Bargain? Nothing could be more pleasant than the Figure he made at this moment. He stood with his Mouth half open, and his Eyes fix'd on her with an unmeaning Stare, all the time she was speaking, nor when she left off, could he either gather up his Countenance, or recollect his Spirits enough to make her any answer; and she went on in this manner: Is this, *said she*, the effect of all the pains I have taken to make you worthy of *Glicera*, and have you given her so many proofs of your Passion, to be found deficient at last, when she was on the very brink of yielding too? — Did she not say last Night, as we were walking together in the Garden, that she thought she had held out long enough against a Person of your Accomplishments and Gallantry, and that there wanted but this one Experiment more to be made of your Generosity, before she threw herself into your Arms. — With what an angelic Softness in her Voice and Eyes did she leaning on my Shoulder, ask me, if I did not think you the most agreea-

---

[51]*Change Alley* the site of deals in stock and gambling speculation (OED).
[52]*chaffer* traffic, trade, buy and sell, deal (OED).

ble Man breathing; — then sigh'd and blush'd: — but I will reveal no more, I will rather persuade her to call back her Heart. — As she was proceeding, the old Sinner, who by this Discourse imagin'd, indeed, that he was belov'd by her: Ah *Laphelia!* *cry'd he out,* do not be so unkind, — she shall have the Mortgage, and I will trust to her Goodness for the Recompence of my Passion; nor did I mean to offend her by those foolish Words, which I beseech you do not report to her, but tell me in what manner this Present will be most acceptable. That indeed requires some thought, *said Laphelia*; and the time you have lost in these idle Scruples, had much better have been employ'd in contriving this handsomely: The manner of conferring an Obligation, is often more than the Obligation itself. — If you give it to her in the fashion you have done a Ring, or Pair of Ear-rings, or some such trifle, I know not if her delicacy will accept it, on the account of the large Sum she knows you have paid down for it; — I would therefore have you do it in the same way as you have enforc'd her, as it were, to take your Money, — that is, lose it at play. — I will pretend to be a little indispos'd, and refuse the Cards: — do you two sit down to *Picquet,*[53] and after you have play'd three or four Games, you may say you have no more ready Money about you, but will set her this Bond against a-Kiss, or some such Favour. — I do not know any thing that will be more truly Gallant, and testify you to have a greater Acquaintance with the *Beau Monde,* than such a Behaviour. — I know you will not leave this Apartment without your Reward, and that I may be no obstacle to your Happiness — as soon as I see the Bond lost, still continuing my feign'd Illness, I will take my Leave, and give you the Liberty of playing on, or making what use you please of the Discovery I have made you after I am gone.

Scarce could the *Alderman* contain his Joy at this Assurance, and now not doubting but that a few Hours would put him in the full possession of what he had so long been labouring to

---

[53] *Picquet* or piquet: a card-game played by two persons with a pack of thirty-two cards (the low cards from the two to the six being excluded) (OED).

obtain, would have fallen on his Knees to thank the obliging
Contriver of his Happiness, if he had not known he must have
put her to the trouble of helping him on his Legs again. — He
utter'd a thousand Expressions of Friendship and Gratitude
after his fashion, and affected to appear so florid, that it was a
task more difficult than any she had yet gone through, for the
Person to whom he addressed himself, to forbear laughing, and
by an ill-tim'd Mirth destroy all she had been doing: But *Glicera*,
who pitied the Constraint she was under, and had been all this
while no farther than the next Room, which being parted from
the other only by a think Wainscot, gave her the Opportunity of
hearing all that had passed; no sooner found her Friend had
succeeded in the Plot they had laid together, than she appear'd,
making a formal Excuse for having stay'd so long. After which
the Cards were call'd for, and the *Ombre*-Table brought; but
Laphelia cry'd her Head ach'd, and she could not play. Let us
have a game at *Picquet* then, Madam, said the *Alderman*. With all
my heart, *reply'd Glicera*, since that ill-natur'd Creature will not
make one among us.

They play'd at first for small Stakes, but the *Alderman* observing Directions to a tittle, pretending he had no more Gold,
pluck'd out the Writings of *Melladore's* Estate, and cry'd, Come
Madam, will you venture a Kiss against this? Yes, answer'd
Glicera, and so begun the Game; *Grubguard* every now and then
looking on *Laphelia*, endeavouring to discover by her Countenance how she approv'd his Behaviour, to which she gave him
an assenting Nod, and he play'd briskly on. — The Game was
soon run off; — *Glicera* had *Point*, or *Quatorze* almost every
time, — and drew the wish'd for Stake; which, as soon as she had
in her Hands, I know not, *said she*, if I have not been playing for
nothing, I understand so little of Law, that I cannot be certain
whether I can demand the Penalty mentioned in this Bond,
without a farther power from you than the bare possession of it.
No, fair *Glicera*, *reply'd the Alderman*, I will not cheat you, and as
you have fairly won it, must also let you know, that before you
can act as *Mortgagee*, there must be a Label annexed to the
Writing, testifying that these Deeds are assign'd to you for a

valuable Consideration receiv'd by me. — I will have a Lawyer then to do it immediately, *said she*, for I love not a Shadow without a Substance. Nor will you feed your Adorer with that airy Food I hope, *resum'd* Grubguard. No, *answer'd she*, to him who truly loves me, I would rather exceed than be any way deficient in the Gratitude I owe him. These words confirming him in the belief which *Laphelia* had before inspir'd him with, made him not in the least oppose her sending for a Lawyer, who happening to live in the same Street, came in a short time, and made *Glicera* as full a *Mortgagee* as if she had pay'd her Money down to *Melladore* for that power.

The Lawyer, as soon as he had done his Business, took his Leave, and *Laphelia*, who stay'd only to set her hand as a Witness, now retired, as she had promised the *Alderman* she would do. Scarce had she left the Room a moment, before the Dotard run to her as fast as Age and Weakness would permit, and began to testify by his Behaviour that he now look'd upon her as his own; but soon did she strike a damp on the Boldness of his aspiring Hopes, her very Looks were sufficient to have aw'd a Lover more emboldened: — Think not, *said she*, to treat me with any other Liberties than such as the chastest Vestal might approve. — It is not in the power of the loveliest, wittiest, and most engaging of all your Sex, to tempt me to an Act of Shame, much less in thine, thou Wretch! worn out with Diseases, bow'd down even to the Grave with Age: — Rather shouldst thou employ the remnant of thy Days in Penitence and Prayer for past Offences, than attempt new ones: — how canst thou, durst thou, think of Sin, when every moment thou hast before thy Eyes unceasing Monitors of thy aproaching Fate? Death and Futurity ought to be now the only Subjects of thy Care, and the vain Pleasures of this World seem odious even to Remembrance. And is it for this, *said he*, that I have parted with so much Money, and the Mortgage of *Melladore*'s Estate! — Did you not tell me that you would not be ungrateful to the Man who truly lov'd you. Yes, *reply'd she*, nor would I be so, were Love and Honour to be found among you; — but you are Betrayers all; — vile Hypocrites! who feign a Tenderness only to undo us. — The

Man who truly *Loves* would *Marry* me; that is not in thy power, already art thou wedded, then what pretence hast thou to a noble Passion: — If I encourag'd thy Addresses, or accepted thy Gifts, 'twas but to punish thy impudent Presumption. — I rais'd thy hopes to make thy Fall from them at once more shocking, and receiv'd thy Presents by way of Payment, for the pains I have taken to reform thee, which sure, if not incorrigible, this Treatment will. — Go home, therefore, and resolve if possible to be honest, and I will then esteem and thank thee for the Benefits thou hast conferr'd upon me; but till then, I look on them only as so many Baits to Shame, and given only to betray my Virtue.

'Twould be needless to say any thing of the Rage of this disappointed Lover, the Reader will easily believe it was excessive; 'tis certain never Man had a greater Shock, and he testifyed his Sense of it in the most bitter Expressions his Capacity would enable him to make; but all he said, having no effect on her, he fell into such railings and revilings, that she was oblig'd to bid him quit the House, and threaten'd that if he stay'd and continued his Incivilities, she would send for those should teach him better Manners.

Thus ended the Amour of old *Grubguard*, and 'tis highly probable that after this he made an attack on no other Woman; for the Mortification he had receiv'd in this, joining with his Age and Infirmities, in a short time sent him to answer in another World the Errors he had been guilty of in this.

Melladore, being in a little time inform'd that *Glicera* was now the *Mortgagee* of his Estate, made use of all the Interest he had in the World, to raise Money to pay it off, having heard too much of the hatred she bore him, and was too conscious of the just Cause he had given her for it, not to expect she would treat him with the utmost Severity. But alas! tho' he had many Relations and Acquaintance, who had it in their *Power* to have oblig'd him, he found none who had the *Will*, and was now by sad Experience convinced that the Unfortunate have few Friends. All his endeavours proving unsuccessful, and his Wife still continuing her Extravagancies, drove him into the greatest Extremities to which a Man can be reduc'd. — He was obliged to

live conceal'd in an obscure part of the Town to avoid being
prosecuted for Debt; — he was in want of almost every Necessary of Life, — and what was more terrible than all besides,
Remorse and late Repentance lash'd his tormented Soul with
ever-during Stings: He was now sensible of, and acknowledged
in Agonies not to be express'd, the Justice of the divine Power in
subjecting him to one he had so greatly wrong'd; he saw the
hand of Heaven was in it, and was so greatly humbled, that, as
much enforc'd by his Griefs for the Baseness he had been guilty
of, as by his Necessities, he writ the following Letter to *Glicera*.

> *To the most deserving, yet most injur'd*
> *of her Sex, the Lovely* GLICERA.

LET not the well-known Characters, which compose this Epistle, I conjure you, put a stop to your perusal of it. — Believe me,
you will find nothing in it of that Disposition which formerly
made me blind to my own Happiness, and throw from me a
Treasure I ought rather to have preserved at the hazard of my
Life. — O *Glicera!* I have greatly wrong'd you, I confess; nor do I
well know whether my Sorrows for the Treatment I have given
you, or for the Misfortunes my Crime has brought upon me,
are the most prevailing in my Soul: — Like the foolish *Indians*, I
have barter'd *Gold* for *Glass*, exchang'd the *best* for one of the
vilest that ever disgraced the name of Woman. — But I imagine
not that my Condition is unknown to you; — the Pawn that you
have in your hands, and which gives you the power over the last
Stake of my ship-wreck'd Fortune, sufficiently informs you to
what a wretched State I am reduc'd. — I will not, therefore,
trouble you with a needless recital of my Misfortunes, my Business now is to implore your Mercy. — Yet, Wretch that I am,
how can I expect or hope for pity from her who found it not
from me. — But Heaven, whom daily we offend, is mov'd by
Penitence and Prayer; and *Glicera* had once so much of the
divine Nature in her, that were I not abandon'd to Despair, and
self-condemn'd, I yet might have some hope in her excelling
Goodness. — I cannot among the great Number of my pretended Friends raise Money to redeem the Mortgage, nor any

part of it; and I am constrain'd to beg you would be pleas'd to release so much of the Land, as I can borrow on, a Sum sufficient to buy a Commission in the Army,[54] and I will make over the Pay to be receiv'd by you till the Debt be discharg'd. — I long to expiate in foreign Wars, the Crimes I have been guilty of at home, and to leave a place in which I have created to myself so much Misery. — I have nothing to urge in my Vindication, nor to move you to a Grant of my Request: — I can only say that I repent, am unhappy, and wholly throw myself on your Goodness, which alone can preserve from a miserable Death

The guilty and undone
MELLADORE.

P.S. I entreat the favour of speedy Answer; for if the hoped Relief arrives not soon, it will be too late to avert the impending and irretrievable Ruin which hangs over my Head.

What more could the most implacable Rage desire, than such a Humiliation! The utmost Malice of the wrong'd *Glicera* was now fully satiated; ample was the Recompence which Heaven allow'd her Injuries, and she acknowledged it, nor wish'd the Offender further Punishment. But tho' her Hatred ceas'd, she persever'd in her Resolution, never to forgive the Treatment she had received from him any otherwise than Christian Charity oblig'd her to do; some of her weak Sex would have again received the Traitor into Favour, and relapsing into the former Fondness by which they had been undone, have thought his Penitence a sufficient Atonement for the Ruin he had caused; but *Glicera* was not of this Humour: Not his most earnest Entreaties, (for after this he sent her several Letters) could prevail on her ever to see him more; she consented however, to let him raise the Sum he requested, which he immediately laid out as he had design'd, and soon after was commanded abroad, whence he return'd no more, being mortally wounded in the first En-

---

[54]*buy a Commission in the Army* A custom that was against the law but widely practiced: the position of an officer in the army could be purchased for a certain sum of money (Ashton, 2:197).

gagement. *Glicera* being in a State of happy Indifference, heard the News of his Death without any Emotions either of Joy or Grief: And having now a sufficient Competency to maintain her for her Life, gave over all Designs on the Men, publickly avowing her Aversion to that Sex; and admitting no Visits from any of them, but such as she was very certain had no Inclinations to make an amorous Declaration to her, either on honourable or dishonourable Terms.

Laphelia, to whose Friendship and ready Wit she was chiefly indebted for her good Fortune, continued to live with her in a fine House, which formerly belong'd to *Melladore*, till the arrival of a young Gentleman to whom she had been a long time contracted, gave her a pleasing Opportunity of quitting her Society, and exchanging the Pleasures of a single Life, for the more careful ones of a married State. *Glicera* loaded her with Presents at her departure, and on all occasions since testifies a Joy, to express the Gratitude with which she regards her. Few Persons continue to live in greater Reputation, or more endeavour by good Actions to obliterate the memory of their past Mismanagement, than does this Fair Jilt; whose Artifices cannot but admit of some Excuse, when one considers the Necessities she was under, and the Provocations she received from that ungrateful Sex.

F I N I S.

THE

DOUBLE MARRIAGE :

OR, THE

FATAL RELEASE.

A   T R U E

Secret **H I S T O R Y.**

Inconstancy's the Plague which first or last

Taints the whole Sex, the catching Court-Disease.

L E E.[55]

---

[55]The epigram is taken from Nathaniel Lee's tragedy, *Mithridates, King of Pontus* (1693), 3.2. Prince Ziphares says these lines about his mistress, Semandra, whom King Mithridates has forcibly taken for his own. Haywood takes these words that are uttered against a woman and uses them against her male protagonist, Bellcour. She slightly misquotes Lee, writing "Inconstancy's" rather than "Inconstancy,".

THE *FATAL RELEASE*

HOW little answerable to the *Beginning* is the *End* of some
People! — And how vainly do we build our Hopes of a *future*
Happiness on the enjoyment of a *present* one! — He that *to-day*
seems *blest* beyond the reach of *Envy*, will, perhaps, *to-morrow* be
wretched, past the relief of *Pity*. — The dark Decrees of *Fate* are
only in the *Execution* to be reveal'd. — There are Events which
cannot be foreseen by *Human* Penetration. — *Wisdom* but vainly
aims to find a Clue, and *Thought* is lost in the mysterious Maze.
Bellcour and *Alathia* set out with so fair a prospect of Prosperity
in Life's uncertain Journey, that few there were who for every
thing cou'd boast the like Advantage: The one was the elder Son
of a Gentleman; no less eminent for his great Possessions than
for the antient and worthy Family from which he was de-
scended. The other was the only Daughter of a Person, who for
Services he had made acceptable to his Country, had been rais'd
above the Gentry, and had something the advantage of the
Father of *Bellcour* in *Grandeur*, as he had the contrary in point of
Wealth. Never were two young Persons more perfect in all the
Accomplishments peculiar to the different Sexes they were of.
Bellcour had as much Learning as was necessary to a Gentleman
who depended not on that alone to raise his Fortune: He had
also admirable Skill in Fencing, and became a Horse as well as
any Man in the World. Musick was a Science in which he took
great delight, and was so great a Master of it, that he compos'd
many excellent Tunes, which were justly admir'd by the best
Proficients in the Art: Nor was he inferior in Dancing to any
Nobleman at Court. To all this, he had an Air and Mien which

gave irresistible Graces to every Thing he said and did: In fine, 'tis impossible to describe him such as he really was; never was Man more form'd to charm. — *Alathia*, on the other hand, had Beauty, such as, in Idea, enliven'd the Fancies of the celebrated *Titian* and *Raphael*,[56] famous for their Representations of the Queen of Love; a Wit no less sparkling than her Eyes, and a Humour the most gay and entertaining that cou'd be, mix'd with a Softness all-inchanting: so engaging was her whole Behaviour, that she seem'd ordain'd only to give Delight, and where-ever she came, inspire an Universal Chearfulness.

These two accomplish'd and lovely Persons from even their very Childhood had been Lovers, and the Intimacy which had ever been between their Families, made the Parents of both observe this growing Passion with pleasure; neither of them having any Reasons, at that time, but to be satisfy'd that such a Tenderness might hereafter be compleated in Marriage. As their Years encreased, so did their mutual Ardors also; and Nature soon informing them what 'twas they long'd for, *Bellcour*, as it was the Business of his Sex, first declar'd the passionate Wishes of his enamour'd Soul, which *Alathia* receiv'd with a modest Contentment in her Eyes; and the pleasing Perturbation of her Thoughts at entering into this new Manner of Conversation, spread a sweet Disorder thro' all her Air and Features, which added fresh Charms to those which had already captivated her transported Adorer. Ah how delightful are the first Emotions of Desire! What gay Ideas does Infant Passion represent! How perfectly happy were now the enamour'd Youth, and melting Maid; but soon, alas! the blissful Dawn was overspread with Clouds of Care, and threatning Storms of Woe. Love had so far overcome the Bashfulness of the fair

---

[56] *Titian and Raphael* Renaissance artists. Titian's most famous works include "The Assumption of the Virgin" (1518), "Sacred and Profane Love" (1510–1512), and "Holy Family with Adoring Shepherd" (1516). Both artists depict personality and spirituality in their portraits rather than mere draftsmanship. Raphael's works reveal a vision of idealized beauty in a harmoniously ordered universe (*Webster's*). Haywood's allusion is meant to emphasize Alathia's beauty, spirituality and intelligence.

Alathia's Nature, that she permitted him to ask the Consent of both their Parents for the Consummation of their mutual Wishes: nor had he any cause to fear a repulse from either, especially from *Maraphill*, so was his Father call'd; having often heard him speak of *Alathia* as of a Person whom he infinitely approv'd of.

Being told he was alone in his Closet, he chose that Opportunity to acquaint him with his Inclinations. He found him busily employed in reading a Letter, the Contents of which seem'd very much to have pleas'd him; and as soon as he perceiv'd his Son *Bellcour*, said he to him with a more than ordinary Chearfulness in his Voice and Eyes: You are come very opportunely, I was about to send for you. — You have often heard me speak of a good old Friend, call'd *Boanarus*; I thought him long since dead, he having left his Country in discontent some Years ago, and taken up his Habitation in *Jamaica*; but, contrary to my hopes or expectations, he is still living, and now on his Voyage home, bringing with him immense Riches, and a Daughter who is his only Child, and they say, the Paragon of her Sex for Beauty and all useful Accomplishments. — But you shall see, *continued he*, what he writes. In speaking these Words, he gave him the Letter; which he no sooner took in his Hands, than he began to tremble, imagining from the first mention of the Daughter of *Boanarus*, what it was that had inspir'd so unusual a Satisfaction in his Father: which Conjecture he was presently confirm'd in, when he read these Lines.

To my very good Friend, the Worthy
MARAPHILL

THAT I writ not to you before, was neither owing to my want of Love, nor a mistrust of yours; but having nothing to acquaint you with for a long time, but a continued Series of Misfortunes, I thought it wou'd denote but little Friendship in me, to put yours to the pain of compassionating those Ills which were no way in your power to ease. — But since Fortune has, at last, blest me with her Smiles, I gladly communicate to you my Affairs. — By some Services I was so happy to do a grateful

Indian,[57] I became so dear to his Esteem, that dying a few Weeks ago, he made me the Heir of all his Wealth, which, in Money and Goods, amounts to no less than 400000 Crowns.[58] — Now, my dear *Maraphill*, I return with pleasure to my native Country, and your more valuable Society; which, without flattery, I assure you, has been the chief Loss I have regretted. — My Girl *Mirtamene*, who you knew a little one, is grown a Woman, and all I have now living of my once numerous Family. — If your Son *Bellcour* has yet escap'd the Snares of *Cupid*, I should rejoice to find him capable of that Passion in her favour; and as what I have, is to descend to her, I should die blest to know the Son of him I most esteem on Earth, the Possessor of it. — I assure you she is such as, without a Parent's Vanity, must be allowed to have as considerable a Share of Beauty as most of her Sex; then for her Education, when in the *worst* of Circumstances, I took care it should be in a manner as might not shame the *best*. — But the Merchant from whose hands you receive this, can give you an exact Account of what she is, and has too great a love for Truth, to flatter her in the Description he shall give you of her. — I wou'd have sent her Picture, but in this Country there are but few Artists. — Besides, you will in a few Months, if the Winds continue favourable, see the Original. — I design to set sail from this Place in a short time; but having this Opportunity, wou'd not omit this brief Recital of what has befallen me: the rest, when we meet, you shall more fully be informed of, by

Your ever faithfully

Affectionate Friend,

and Humble Servant,

BOANARUS.

What was now the Emotions which fill'd the Soul of this enarmour'd Youth, at News which he foresaw wou'd be so kill-

---

[57] *Indian* relating to the race of original inhabitants of America and the West Indies, but also referring to a European, especially an Englishman, who resides or has resided in India or the Indies (OED).

[58] *400000 Crowns* £100,000.

ing to his Desires, and the unchangeable Affection he had vow'd
Alathia! His inward Confusion burst out in such visible Tokens,
that *Maraphill* cou'd not but take notice of it; and changing on a
sudden that Countenance of Serenity which he had worn a
moment before, into one wholly the reverse: What, Son, *demanded he, in an angry Accent*, are you disturb'd at that which
rather shou'd give you the most exquisite Satisfaction? — Do you
not look on this Offer as a Blessing sent from Heaven? — A
Lady of such Beauty, Wit, and Wealth thrown by Providence
into your Arms. — 'Sbud![59] were I a young Fellow, I shou'd be
transported at the Thoughts. — I have spoke to the Merchant
mention'd in the Letter, and he tells me that *Mirtamene* is the
Wonder of the World. She may be so, Sir! *humbly reply'd* Bellcour; but you know that where the Heart is already taken up,
all other Charms are ineffectual: — The Beauties of *Alathia* have
done the Work of all her Sex, nor is it in the power of any other
Woman to erase the Impression she has made. Very well, *interrupted the old Gentleman, extremely incens'd*; but do you not remember that your Heart ought to have been at my disposal? — How
dare you then to make a Present of it without having first
consulted me? Love is an involuntary and resistless Passion,
said the troubled Son, and were the Object of it in every thing my
Inferior, I know not if all the Precepts of Duty, or of Interest,
wou'd have been sufficient to have restrain'd the growing
Flame; but such as *Alathia* is, so worthy of Adoration, so much
beyond what any Man can merit, I had not the least Cause to
doubt your Approbation of my Choice, and without making
even the least Effort to repel the sweet Invasion, suffer'd her
Charms to take possession of my Soul; and it is now so wholly
hers, so truly devoted to her, that Heaven itself wants Power to
work a Change. How vain wou'd be all Endeavours to represent
that Rage which at the boldness of this Declaration swell'd the
Breast of *Maraphill!* He upbraided the Ingratitude and impudent Presumption, as he call'd it, of his Son, in Terms the most

[59]*'Sbud!* an oath; a further shortening of the euphemistic shortening of "God's
bodikins" or "God's dear body!" (OED).

111

severe that Tongue cou'd utter, and finding that all he said
serv'd rather to strengthen than any way abate the Resolution
he had taken, of continuing firm to the Vows he had made
Alathia, he bid him quit his Presence, and see him no more till
he had better learned his Duty: on which, *Bellcour*, making a low
Bow, obey'd, saying only as he left the Room, that he might
break, by his unkindness, the Strings which held his Heart, but
never make it false to his for-ever dear *Alathia*. 'Tis difficult to
say whether the Father or the Son thought themselves most
unhappy after this Conversation; the one thought it a Hardship
not to be sustain'd with patience, that a Son of whose Education
he had taken so much Care, and whom he had lov'd with a
Tenderness infinitely superior to what the greatest part of Parents express, shou'd not in all Things be conformable to his
Will. The *other* look'd on it as the utmost Rigour of his Fate, that
there was a Power on Earth capable of controuling him in
Desires which appear'd so reasonable; and tho' he had ever been
accustom'd to behave with the utmost *Duty*, resolved now to be
disobedient, and thought the *breach* of it a less Crime than *Falshood* or *Ingratitude* to a Mistress, to whom he so often had vow'd
an everlasting Faith, and by whom he knew himself to be most
tenderly belov'd. The Case indeed on both sides was hard, and
scarce can one blame either the *Resentment* of the *Father*, or the
Resolution of the *Son*, tho' both might have behav'd with greater
Moderation; but *Passion* has small regard to *Reason*, and the
different ones, with which these two were agitated, were at
present too violent to leave room for Consideration in the
Breast of either.

Bellcour flew immediately to *Alathia*, and acquainted her with
their Misfortune in Terms so moving and so tender, as left her
no cause to suspect either the Beauty of her Rival, or his Father's Power wou'd have any effect to make him swerve from
that Affection he had sworn to her: foreseeing, however, the
Difficulties which wou'd attend their Love, and the almost impossibility there was that they should ever be happy; she endeavour'd to persuade him to a Forgetfulness of her, and a
Resignation to his Father's Will: but, alas! all she said on this

Head was utter'd with so faint an Accent, and with so little
Spirit urg'd, that it was easy to be discover'd how vastly different from the Dictates of her Heart was the Language of her
Tongue. Had *Bellcour* but seem'd to give into her Reasons, or
but listen'd to them with any show of Consent, 'tis probable the
cruel Adherence had been fatal, with so unspeakable a Passion
did she regard him: but there was no danger of her being put to
that Trial; the enflam'd *Bellcour* could not support this Discourse, a hundred times he interrupted the few Arguments she
alledg'd, call'd her Unkind and Cruel, and question'd her Love
in such a manner, as wou'd have entirely remov'd all Suspicion
of his Truth, if she had been capable to have entertain'd any. —
Ah, *Alathia! cry'd he,* can you pretend to love, yet wish the Object
of your Affections for ever lost! — Nay more, *continued he,* can
you pretend even Friendship to the Man you wish a Villain!–
Have I not sworn, have I not vow'd a thousand, thousand
times, I liv'd but for *Alathia,* and wou'd chuse Death rather than
Falshood! — No, may just Heaven forsake me, load me with
Curses here, and at the Hour of my Death, when most I pray
and cry for Mercy, may it be deaf, and not one Saint convey my
penitential Sighs, but plunge me down in endless Woe and
ever-during Hell, a Companion for Fiends, whenever I become
like them, as I must do, to deviate even in Thought from thee;
thou Soul of Sweetness, thou lovely Abstract of all that's good in
Woman! — By these kind of Imprecations did he put a stop to
every thing she was about to say, till she was oblig'd to tell him,
no Misfortune cou'd be so dreadful to her as that of his being
false. They then swore together an eternal Fidelity, each wish-
ing the most unheard of Curses on themselves, if ever they were
guilty of a breach of it. In this tender, but melancholy Conversation, they continued for many Hours, not parting till it was
very late at Night, and not then without an Assurance of meeting the next Day.

But little did they think, that while by these mutual Promises
to each other, they were endeavouring to combat with their ill
Stars, and baffle the Decrees of Fate, what was in those Moments acting against their Love. *Maraphill,* full of the Indigna-

tion which the Reply of *Bellcour* had inspir'd him with, happen'd, by Accident, to meet the Father of *Alathia*, whom accosting with a Countenance very much the contrary of that he had been accustomed to put on to him; I am told, *said he to him*, that there is a Love-affair carry'd on between your Daughter and my Son, I know not if you are privy to it; but can assure you, I was entirely ignorant such a thing was in agitation till this Day, else had before acquainted you that I have otherwise dispos'd of *Bellcour*, and shou'd he be refractory to the Choice I have made, shall wholly cast him off. — It will be prudence in you, therefore, not to encourage his too frequent Visits at your House, which, as they are made without my Leave, can terminate in no other Consequence than the dishonour of your Daughter. 'Tis difficult to say whether Surprize or Disdain was more predominant in the Mind of him to whom these Words were address'd; he knew the Passion which *Bellcour* profess'd for his Daughter, and was also sensible the other cou'd not have been a Stranger to it: the Equality of their Fortunes and Parity of Humours, had made him think there wou'd be no Objections to the Marriage. These Words, therefore, so unexpected, and abrupt, made him extremely wonder what had occasion'd the sudden Alteration: the greatness of his Spirit wou'd not, however, suffer him to desire an Explanation, and, by the Example of the other, throwing off all that Freedom with which they had been used to treat each other; if your Son be amorous of *Alathia*, *reply'd he*, there is nothing in it very surprizing, nor is it so, that if I have taken notice of it I shou'd not acquaint you, because I doubted not but what he did was by your permission: — but whether it be so or not, I shall not fail to oblige you in forbidding my Daughter to receive his Visits; nor need I question her Obedience in this point, while I am in a Condition, such as will keep her above the Necessity of being reduc'd to steal a Marriage,[60] or to ask pardon of the Family into which she weds, before she can be receiv'd into it. He had no sooner spoke this,

---

[60]*to steal a Marriage* to get married secretly (clandestinely) without publishing the banns; marrying without a licence.

114

than he flung from the Place, leaving *Maraphill* very well satisfy'd at this breach of their former Friendship, and the assurance
that his Pride wou'd certainly make him do as he had said, tho'
it were to the breaking of his Daughter's Heart. Happening
afterwards into other Company, he came not home till *Bellcour*
was departed, and his Daughter gone to Bed; but early in the
Morning he sent for her into his Chamber, and charg'd her
strictly to see *Bellcour* no more; relating to her, at full, the Discourse he had with his Father, and bidding her know herself
better than to receive the Addresses of a Man, whose Family
look'd on them as an Honour to her. The young Lady fainted
away at this Injunction of her Father's, yet had nothing to offer
in contradiction to it, only intreated the Liberty of telling *Bellcour* himself the Occasion of the Change she must henceforward
observe in her Behaviour to him. It was with some difficulty
that the old Gentleman granted this Request; but the trouble he
was in to see her thus afflicted, and the respect he had for
Bellcour, who he found had no share in what his Father did, at
last prevail'd upon him.

What was now the Meeting of these unhappy Lovers! *Alathia*
receiv'd the wondring *Bellcour* with streaming Eyes, and such a
Storm of Sighs, as wou'd not, for some moments, allow her the
liberty of Speech: Silent a-while both stood, he fear'd to ask
what she as yet had not the power of revealing; struggling, at
last, tho' half suffocated with the rising Grief, she brought forth
in stammering and scarce intelligible Accents, Oh, *Bellcour! Bellcour!* I must see you no more. — Take now your everlasting
Leave of lost *Alathia!* — She said no more, the Efforts she had
made to utter this, exhausted the small Stock of Grief, the over-
powring Passion had left her Mistress of; and she fell fainting in
her Lover's Arms. To conceive what it was that *Bellcour* felt at
the hearing Words like these, and the Condition to which the
speaking of them had reduc'd the Person, who, at that time, was
a thousand times dearer to him than his Life; one must be
possess'd of all the various and perplexing Passions, which de-
throne Reason, and torment Humanity. — His less soft Nature
refusing him the ease of Tears, with wild Distraction his whirl-

ing Brain turn'd round. — His Bosom swell'd almost to bursting; his Heart was torn with Anguish unutterable! unsupportable! He rav'd, he tore his very Flesh; nay, even, roar'd out with the extremity of Pain. — 'Tis certain, that at this cruel moment, Whips, Racks, or scalding Sulphur,[61] were Tortures inferior to those he suffer'd. But *Alathia* recovering from her Swoon, and beholding him thus, a-while seem'd to forget her own Despair, to mitigate the Pangs of his. With Expressions compos'd of the most endearing Softness, did she endeavour to recall his wandring Reason, and restore him to Tranquility. — 'Tis true, *said she*, I am forbid by him whom yet I never disobey'd, to hear your Vows, receive your Ardors, or even to see you more; but, oh my *Bellcour!* Love is superior to all the Precepts of Duty, and of Prudence. I cannot *live* in an eternal Absence from you; nor can I *die* while I perceive my Life of so much moment to your Peace. — Yes, yes, in spite of all our cruel Fathers can do, we will not, must not be separated. — Oh! therefore give not way to this impatient Rage, but rather, while we have the blessed Opportunity, contrive some Way by which we may be just to the Oath we mutually have taken. These last Words resettled some part of that Composure in his Mind, which his late Disorders seem'd entirely to have banish'd; and looking stedfastly on her, Divine *Alathia, said he*, how unworthy is the Son of such a mercenary Father, to receive this heavenly Goodness! — Let us talk no more, *interrupted she*, of either of our Fathers, but think what is best for us to do, to avert the Ruin they intend to bring upon our Love. What possibility is there, *return'd he*, but, by giving the Church's Sanction to the Marriage of our Hearts, put it past their power to divide us more? But then a Father's Curse, *said she*, I tremble when I think what Woes offended Heaven denounces against a Breach of Duty to those to whom we owe

---

[61] *Racks, or scalding Sulphur rack*: an instrument of torture formerly in use, consisting (usually) of a frame having a roller at each end; the victim was fastened to these by the wrists and ankles, and had the joints of his limbs stretched by their rotation (OED); *scalding sulphur*: in popular belief sulphur has been associated with the fires of hell, devils and thunder and lightning (OED).

our Being; besides, were there a Hope that Sin could be ab-
solved, by what unhoped Means cou'd we award the threatning
Stings of Want! how shun the World's Derision, when Poverty
with all her mean Attendants sits at our unfrequented Doors,
and frights the wary Passenger from Entrance! — Should we not
sit alone unaided, unfriended, expos'd to Shame, to Censure?
and who can tell but when thus Desolate, thus forsaken of all,
but even we ourselves may join with Fortune, and add to our
own Misery by a too late Repentance; and regretting the fond
Folly which brought us to this Wretchedness, upbraid by turns
each other? Oh never! never! cry'd Bellcour, cou'd I be guilty of
such Baseness, much less cou'd thy angelick Nature descend to
mean Reproach, or poor Reviling: But tho' I could be content,
for thee, to suffer all the Woes which formful Fancy can invent,
yet cou'd I not support the Thought of any Ill befalling thee. —
The Secret of our Marriage must, therefore, be with Care conceal'd; nor think that when a Husband's Name shall give me
power over thy Beauties, I will require the Possession of them,
but at such times as when *Argus*-Ey'd Suspicion[62] shall be lull'd
asleep, and I unseen, unthought of, may securely steal to thy
dear Arms. — Thus for a while we may delude the busy Care of
our too cruel Parents; and while they think us most at *distance*,
be as *near* as Hope can ask. — Who knows what Revolutions may
hereafter happen in our Affairs? — A sad one lately has arriv'd,
another may ensue to make us yet more *blest*, than this has
made us *wretched*. To these he added many other Arguments to
persuade her to yield to his Desires, and as every thing he said
seem'd dictated by the fondest Passion, and the strictest Honour; too well she *lov'd*, to be capable of refusing him, and it was
agreed between them, that she should pretend to her Father to
have done as he commanded her; and that the very next Morning after the ensuing Day, she should meet him at a Shop where
she used sometimes to buy Things, and to which if she should
happen to be watched, there wou'd be no Suspicion of the intent

---

[62]*Argus-Ey'd Suspicion* extremely watchful or sharp-sighted. Argus was a mythological person fabled to have had one hundred eyes.

for which she came, and that from thence they shou'd take Coach and go to the House of a Divine, who on the account of some Affairs relating to the Publick had been suspended,[63] and who was well known to *Bellcour*; and after he had join'd their Hands, each to return to their respective Habitations, to the end that no Mistrust might arise of their having been together, in either of their Families.

Alathia play'd her Part so well, tho' it was her first Task of Hypocrisy, that her Father was entirely deceiv'd by it; and having ever found her most obedient to his Will in all things, did not doubt but she would continue so in this, tho' he believ'd she cou'd not be so without reluctance, and which indeed she feign'd, the better to delude him, and prevent him from having too observing an Eye over her Actions for the future. *Bellcour*, altho' a Man (strange Paradox!) was less successful in Dissimulation; but he had not yet learn'd the Practices of his betraying Sex, and was not half perfect in the undoing Art: he had never made professions of Love to any but *Alathia*, and as they were sincere, and tended only to the attainment of his Wishes on honourable Terms; he stood not in need of trying his Skill that way: the Pleasure he conceived at disappointing all the Measures which cou'd be taken to deprive him of his adorable Mistress, was too great to be conceal'd, in spite of his Efforts to the contrary; the secret Satisfaction smil'd in his Eyes, and sat triumphant on each Feature of his Face. *Maraphill* who by his Behaviour to him in the Closet, and what he had learn'd by his Deportment since by the Servants, expected to have seen in him the most evident Tokens of Despair; was so much surpriz'd when he perceiv'd him the contrary, that he cou'd not but imagine there was a Motive for it more than he knew, or shou'd be pleas'd with: He therefore order'd all his Actions shou'd be observ'd with the utmost diligence, and every Motion watch'd;

[63]*a Divine. . .had been suspended* A clergyman could be suspended for three years by the church authorities for conducting a clandestine marriage (a marriage without a licence). Suspension "virtually forced him into conducting more [secret marriages] in order to survive" (Stone, 27).

which being accordingly done, he was seen to go into that Shop, and soon after take Coach with *Alathia*. This Account put him into the utmost perplexity, and he resolv'd some way or other to disappoint their future Meetings; but how, he cou'd not yet determine. *Bellcour* in the mean time was in little less perplexity; 'tis true, he was *married* to the Charmer of his Soul, but *Consummation* had not past, that dear Reward of his long suffering Passion was yet to come, and his impatient Wishes for that happy Moment, render'd him little less disorder'd than the Emotions of his Despair had done. But *Alathia*, who on parting from him, had promis'd to contrive some Means to see him soon again, forgot not what she had said: and counterfeiting an excessive Melancholy, entreated leave of her Father to retire into the Country. Change of Place, *she told him*, affording variety of Objects, might obliterate the Memory of the old ones, and enable her in time to forget *Bellcour*, which it was impossible she shou'd do while she continued where every Thing she saw wou'd serve but to remind her of him. This Request appear'd too reasonable to be refus'd, and every Thing was prepared with all convenient speed for her removal. *Bellcour*, for whose sake she had contriv'd this Stratagem, was inform'd of it by a Letter she found means of conveying to him; and also the Method she wou'd have him take, to prevent any discovery of their Correspondence, or the Visits he shou'd make her in that Retirement to which she was going. She had formerly been at the House of a Relation, which she remembred to have stood in a By-lane, a good distance from any other: the nearest in the Neighbourhood was an Inn; this was the Place she made choice of, because she thought that *Bellcour*, as well as other Passengers, might sometimes take up his Lodgings in that Inn, and they might have the Opportunity of indulging their mutual Wishes with each other's Society, as often as he could make a pretence to stay from home all Night. The Father of this tender Bride having little Suspicion of the Deceit she had put upon him, sent her without any other Company than such as she should find in the Stage Coach, knowing there were Servants sufficient to attend her where she was going, and also because she seem'd not to be very well pleased with the Maid who at present waited on her; and told him she would hire one to her own mind in the Country, where there were many Farmers Daughters who wou'd be glad to serve her. Of this the joyful Bridegroom being appriz'd, met her at the Inn where she was to lie; and receiving her with all the Transports of the most unfeigned Affection, secure and uninterrupted, took possession of his Right, and made *Alathia* now indeed a Wife. All Night they past in Joys which none but happy Lovers know; but proportion'd to the Bliss they had shar'd, was their mutual disquiet, when the unwelcome Morn reminded them that they must part. — The Coach got ready very early, and the late transported Pair had their tender Adieus cut off by the rude Summons of the too hasty Driver. *Alathia* arriv'd in a few hours safe at the House of her Cousin, where she was welcom'd with the utmost chearfulness, and *Bellcour* rid back to Town; far from imagining his Father knew he had been from home all Night, having charg'd all the Family not to let him into the Secret.

But he had not been in the House half an Hour before he found he had been deceiv'd in his Conjecture. With a Storm on his Brow did the angry *Maraphill* accost him, told him he was perfectly well acquainted with his Proceedings, and that he was truly inform'd, that in spite of his positive Commands to the contrary, he had continued his former Pretensions to *Alathia*. He utter'd these Accusations with so assur'd an Air, that *Bellcour* doubted not but that every Thing he had done was known to him, and thinking all denials would be vain, imagin'd it would be better he shou'd believe he had been guilty of it, *before* than *since* the Knowledge of his aversion to it. How impossible was it for me, Sir, *said he*, to foresee your good Thoughts of *Alathia* shou'd so suddenly alter and become the very Reverse of what they had been! — I hope you will not, therefore, think it a Crime too great to be forgiven, if presuming on your Goodness, and confident of your Approbation, the violence of my Passion made those Promises which I confess shou'd, in the first place, have been authoriz'd by you. 'Sdeath, what Promises! *interrupted the old Man fiercely*, you are

120

not sure contracted? — And then by his silence, guessing the worst; Heavens! 'tis not impossible but that you may be married! — but if you have dar'd to treat me in this manner, by all that we adore above, or fear below, thou art an Alien to my Family and Name; never will I see thee, but with Horror, nor mention thee but with Curses. — Oh all ye Powers! *continued he*, if *Bellcour* be the Husband of *Alathia*, let every kind of Mischief fall upon him, let Poverty and Shame be the least of Evils that shall attend him; but *Guilt* be added to his *Wretchedness*, Fiends haunt his Steps, and sudden Death overtake him, and plunge him deep in ever-during Hell. How terrible were Words like these, proceeding from a *Father's* Mouth! The Soul of *Bellcour* shrunk back with Horror, and wild Confusion sat on all his Form; the Disorders he perceiv'd in him, together with his Silence, made *Maraphill* believe what was indeed the Truth; and transported with the most vehement Indignation that ever enter'd the Heart of Man, he drew his Sword, and taking him by the Throat, utter'd unheard of Imprecations on himself, if he did not, that moment, plunge it in his Breast, unless he spoke, and inform'd him of the depth of his Engagements with *Alathia*; yet at the same time renewing his Curses on him, if he had proceeded too far to be recall'd. It was not the Fear of *Death*, but the eternal *Displeasure* of a *Father* to whom he had all the duteous Regard that Son cou'd pay, which so long depriv'd him of the power of Utterance, and made him now not dare avow the Truth. Throwing himself on his Knees, he entreated him to moderate his Rage, protesting to him in the most solemn manner, that nothing in the World cou'd be so dreadful to him as the thoughts of offending so good a Parent; but still evading any direct Answer to the Question propos'd to him: which instead of abating, encreas'd both the Doubt and Vexation of *Maraphill*. To the utmost pitch of Extravagance did the Tempest of his Passion hurry him, and again demanding of him if he were married or not, he repeated those Curses with redoubled Fury, which he had before pronounced if he were. I am not married, *answered the trembling* Bellcour, *faintly*, any otherwise than in the Wishes of my devoted Heart. Then I again receive thee to my Love, *resum'd his Father*, and will take care to put it out of even thy own power ever to forfeit it. — You must resolve, *continu'd he, going to the Door, and bringing in a Person whom till that moment* Bellcour *had never seen*, to go with this Gentleman where he shall conduct you by my Orders. — He will find means of diverting the Folly of the present Passion of your Soul, and render it fit for that more noble one, the charming *Mirtamene* at her arrival cannot fail of inspiring. What was now the Condition of this unhappy Lover, this distracted Husband? From this Destiny there was no Reprieve. *Maraphill* continuing his Discourse, told him he must be gone that very Hour, that unknown to him he had taken care to have his Clothes pack'd up, and provided Horses, Servants, and all Conveniencies for him, and that he wou'd allow no longer time than wou'd suffice to ask his Blessing, till he began his Journey. 'Tis utterly impossible to describe the present Conflict in the Thoughts of poor *Bellcour*, such as it was in reality. — More than once did he open his Mouth to reveal the whole Truth, and confess that he had deceived him; but the remembrance of his late Rage, and those heart-rending Curses he had laid upon him, deterr'd him from doing it. In the midst of the most terrible Disorders the Mind can know, sometimes a ready Thought presents itself; *Bellcour* had now one which flatter'd him with a View of Success, and made him imagine wou'd be an Expedient to deliver him from this Exigence. Having a little paus'd upon it, he entreated the favour of *Maraphill* to have his private Ear for something he had to communicate of the greatest Importance; to which he consenting, desir'd the Gentleman, who was to be the Guardian of his Son, to leave the Room. On which, Tho' the Ceremony of the Church, *said he*, has not yet past between *Alathia* and myself, yet since you are return'd to a Disposition, which encourages me to confess the Truth, I must inform you, Sir, that the most solemn Vows have past between us, and that not only my own Conscience forbids me to be the Husband of another, but also that the Promises I have made her, are of such a nature, as if broke, wou'd render me liable to Punishment by an earthly

Court.[64] — Tut, *reply'd the old Man*, the Law takes no Cognizance of a *Verbal* Contract;[65] — I hope she has nothing under your Hand. Both Hand and Seal have made it firm and valid, *resum'd the other*, and no less than the Forfeit of the whole Estate which on your Death descends to me, is the Penalty, if without her consent I wed another: — How impossible is it therefore to obey you? — For I protest so truly am I touched with a just Sense of my Crime in entring into this Engagement without having first receiv'd Permission from you; that all the Tenderness I have for *Alathia*, cannot absolve, or make me not repent it. If this be true, *said* Maraphill, *more troubled, but less incens'd than he had been*, perhaps when she shall know how little I am able to endure the thoughts of this Alliance, and the Revenge I have sworn to take on you whenever you shall dare make good what you have promis'd, she will be prevail'd on to resign the Power your Folly has given [her] over [you]. Doubt it not, Sir, *resum'd* Bellcour, (*glad to find his Father come so readily into the Imposition he was putting on him*) I am not by the Contract bound to marry her, but not to be the Husband of another; the same Obligation too is laid on her, and when she shall be told how impossible it is she ever shou'd be mine, she doubtless will rejoice to be deliver'd from a restriction no way agreeable to her Youth and Beauty: — Permit me, therefore, *pursued he*, once more to visit her, and by revealing to her the Truth of this Affair, regain my Liberty, and restore hers. *Maraphill* stood in

---

[64]*Promises. . .Punishment by an eartly Court* Bellcour here implies that he has made a verbal contract with Alathia which was legally binding prior to 1753 if "a man and a woman over the age of consent (14 and 12)," exchanged vows, "witnessed by two persons, and expressed in the present tense. A promise made in the future tense, however, was only binding if it was followed by consummation, which was taken to be evidence of consent in the present" (Stone, 17). After Maraphill tells Bellcour that "the Law takes no Cognizance of a Verbal Contract," Bellcour adds that it was written and "Both Hand and Seal have made it firm and valid."

[65]*Verbal Contract* Although "in church law a verbal contract, performed in the present tense before witnesses was complete in substance. . .and was indissoluble. . .in common law. . .and therefore in all matters relating to property, the contract had no standing whatever" (Stone, 18).

a fix'd Posture, intently observing him all the time he had been speaking, and perceiving nothing in his Countenance which cou'd give him room to doubt the truth of what he said, agreed to his Request, and told him he should defer it no longer than the next Day; but that to prevent him from making any other use of the Opportunity he allow'd him of seeing her, than such as he pretended; he must consent that the Person whom he had just now seen, shou'd accompany him so near the House where she was, that no Person cou'd go in or out without his knowledge. To which *Bellcour* was not at all averse; but having assur'd his Father that he wou'd say and do every thing that was proper to engage her to give up the Contract; he told him, that he hoped he after would not insist on his leaving him, protesting that in all his Life he had never felt so sensible a grief, as that which the Thoughts of being banished from his Presence had involv'd him in. To which *Maraphill* reply'd, that on his Honour he shou'd not.

By the whole Behaviour of *Bellcour*, and what had been said of the passionate Tenderness, with which, from even his Childhood, he had regarded *Alathia*; it cannot be imagin'd that he had any other meaning in this than to gain time, and prevent his Father from sending him to some Place where it would be impossible for him either to see, or send to her; and he related what had pass'd with so much Sincerity, that she had not the least cause to doubt of his Affection; nor that he had any other Design in what he requir'd of her, than by lulling asleep the Fears and Watchfulness of *Maraphill*, they might for the future enjoy the Society of each other without interruption, or the danger of being for ever separated. Having therefore an implicite Faith in the Love and Honour of her dear Husband, and unable to support the Thoughts of his being remov'd from her to a Place of which she was wholly ignorant, and where it was not to be doubted but that he wou'd be too vigilantly watch'd, to have any Opportunity of even sending to her; the Joys his *Presence* yielded, join'd to the terrors of a long *Absence*, made her hesitate but a very little to sign a Release from all former Contracts and Obligations. He told her, that now there wou'd be no danger of his being compell'd to leave the Town, and for that reason entreated she wou'd return to it as soon as possible, because being so near, he cou'd have many Opportunities of seeing her at some House which he wou'd hereafter contrive; which, while she was at so great a distance, was not possible to be done without Suspicion, or perhaps a Discovery, to the total Ruin of their Love. She having assur'd him of her ready Compliance with his Will, he took his leave; and finding the Gentleman, who had accompany'd him, waiting in a Field within a Bow-shot of the House, they return'd home together; where *Bellcour* showing the Release, was joyfully receiv'd by his Father. For two days, he had not the least reason but to be satisfy'd with what he had done. He had his liberty to go where he pleas'd, had no Spies sent after him, as heretofore, and doubted not but all the Jealousies of *Maraphill* were now lull'd asleep; but how strangely was he surpriz'd, when on the third he saw the Coach and Six come to the Door, several Horses for the Servants to ride upon, a vast deal of Luggage pack'd up, and all necessary Preparations made for a long Journey! As he was debating in his Mind what could be the reason for it, or who it was that was about to travel, his Father came into the Room, where he was looking out of the Window, and taking him by the Hand, *Bellcour, said he*, I am going into the Counry for some time, you must accompany me some part of the Way. The Colour of *Bellcour* chang'd two or three times, while *Maraphill* was speaking these few Words: but not daring to refuse a Command which seem'd so reasonable; May I presume, Sir, *said he*, to ask the Cause which has induced you to so unexpected a removal? I will inform you as we go, *answer'd the Father*, and immediately stept into the Coach, where he was follow'd by his astonish'd Son, and presently after by that old Gentleman who had been recommended as a Governour to *Bellcour*, and who had accompany'd him in the Visit he made to *Alathia*. The sight of him gave something of a shock to *Bellcour*, tho' at that time he could not account for it. But long did he not remain in Suspence: When they were past the Town a few Miles; Now Son, *said* Maraphill *to him*, I will reveal to you, what hitherto the Fears of your

125

foolish Passion for *Alathia* has oblig'd me to keep a Secret. — You are now on your Journey to a Place whence till you are the Husband of *Mirtamene* you must not expect to return: — Not that I will break my Word with you; I promis'd that if you procur'd your Liberty from *Alathia*, I wou'd not banish you my Presence; and to the end, that I may keep it inviolably, I go with you: — but do not imagine that I believ'd you enough cured of that Disobedience you formerly avowed, as to trust you in a City where you might every Hour have an Opportunity of disappointing my Designs. — The Release you have from *Alathia* discharges you from all past Engagements, but does not imply but you may hereafter enter into others, perhaps, more destructive to my Hopes: I have therefore taken this only infallible Way to put it beyond your power to contradict my Will and your own good Fortune; which I doubt not but I shall hear you, one day, acknowledge depends on the Possession of that accomplish'd young Lady I have made choice of for you. He had no sooner left speaking, than the old Gentleman began a long Discourse on the Duty of Children to their Parents, and how little capable Youth was, especially when blinded by Passion, of knowing what was best for them. *Bellcour*, who for some time had been prevented from interrupting him by the strange mixture of his Thoughts, had now no longer Patience; but looking on him with the utmost fierceness, bid him be silent, telling him that however the Duty of a Son might oblige him to offer nothing in opposition to what a Father said, yet he knew of no Motive which should oblige him to listen to such Remonstrances from any other Person. *Maraphill*, unwilling to exasperate him, prevented the other from returning any thing which might have done it, by assuring him that he should find nothing but what might serve to divert him. To represent the perplexity which this unhappy Lover now found himself involv'd in, would be as impossible, as it is to give to painted Flames the same Force as the Reality with fatal Scorchings boasts: The imprison'd Passions warring in his Breast, struggled for vent, and scarce cou'd be restrain'd by all the Considerations of Duty, Interest or Affection. — He did, however, gain so much the power over them, as not to utter the least Word at which his Father cou'd take Offence; but in his sullen Looks his Discontent too plainly was discover'd for him to have conceal'd it, if he had attempted it. — This gave an alarm to *Maraphill*, and made him not only think that he had done well in removing, but also that it was necessary to watch him with the utmost Care, lest he should escape from the Place where they were going, and return to *Alathia*; and all the time of their Journey, which was five Days, he never suffer'd him one moment from his Sight, obliging him to lie in the same Chamber, and never quit his Presence on any pretence whatsoever. Nor when they were arriv'd at the House, which he had privately hir'd for this Purpose, did he in the least abate his former Vigilance, keeping him still in his own Eye, or that of the old Gentleman who came with them.

This Retreat was in a little Village near one of the most considerable Sea-ports of the Kingdom, and where in all proba- bility *Boanarus* wou'd land, it being the first Harbour in his way from *Jamaica*. It was therefore the design of *Maraphill* to be there ready to receive him, and see the Marriage celebrated before he returned to the Metropolis. *Bellcour* soon perceived his Inten- tion, but tho' his inventive Brain was ever on the Rack to find out some Means to evade it without discovering the Truth, yet did nothing present itself which appear'd possible to be accom- plish'd; that which he thought most feasible, was to acquaint the young Lady, in private, with the Secret of his Marriage, and the terrible Curse his Father had laid on him, if he refus'd to obey him, and then entreat she wou'd commiserate his unhappy Cir- cumstance, and by openly declaring a dislike to him, take from him the blame of breaking off. This it was that he resolved to do the first Opportunity he had of speaking to her after her Ar- rival, which now was every day expected.

Maraphill, who, as he had said, did all that was possible to make this retirement supportable to his Son, and to obliterate the Memory of *Alathia*, contriv'd one Day a great Hunting- match, to which all the Gentlemen for many Miles round the Country were invited. *Bellcour* had always been a great lover of this Diversion; but the Pleasure he now conceived at hearing it design'd, sprung from a different Cause than meerly the Sport which the rest of the Company propos'd to themselves: He had hopes that in the eagerness of following the Chace, he might have the Opportunity of escaping those more than *Argus*-Eyes, which had continually been a Spy upon him, and that he might cross the Country, and by unfrequented Roads be past the search of any who shou'd be sent in pursuit of him, and get to some place where he might conceal himself till the Danger of marrying *Mirtamene* should be over; believing with reason, that a young Lady of her reported Beauty, Fortune, and Accomplishments, cou'd not hear what he had done to avoid marrying, without being possess'd of a disdain for him, which would oblige her to refuse him, if offer'd to her afterwards. He was not deceiv'd in some part of his Conjecture; they started variety of Game, and the Company dividing into different Parties, he easily rode from his Observers; and *Maraphill* believing he was with the old Gentleman, and he, thinking he was in company with his Father, neither made any Enquiry after him, for a long time. In the mean while, he had cross'd several Roads, and was got into a Wood, some 10 or 12 Miles distant from the Hunters; passing along then more slowly than he had done, he began to deliberate within himself which way it was best for him to direct his Course, or whether he had any Friend in the World to whom he cou'd apply himself for refuge, till the time of his Father's displeasure should be over, or if it were not better to conceal himself among Strangers. As he was in this Dilemma, he heard a Woman's Voice in the most terrible Shrieks that ever pierc'd his Ears; looking about him to see if he cou'd discover from whom they came, he spy'd two Horses, one of which, by the Furniture,[66] he knew to belong to one of the Female Sex, the other had on it a Man's Saddle; but both being richly accoutred, made him not doubt but that they belong'd to some Persons of distinction, and that there was some extraordinary Piece of Villany in hand: Being naturally generous and brave, he clapt

---

[66]*Furniture* equipment, personal belongings; in this case, a woman's side-saddle.

Spurs to his Horse, and gallop'd towards the Place whence the Cry proceeded. Still as he drew nearer he heard the Voice more plain, and at last, to his great Amazement, saw a Man well habited, but with a Devil-like Fierceness in his Countenance, holding by the Hair a young Maid of such exquisite Beauty, that, till his Eyes were witness of it, he could not have believ'd had been in Nature; the darling Whiteness of her delicate Skin, which her torn Robes disclos'd in greater measure than else her Modesty would have permitted; her shining Eyes sparkling with Rage, her fine form'd Mouth, her lovely Hair which the *Barbarian* had wound round his remorseless Hand, her Shape, her Stature, and that heavenly Innocence and Softness, which, even in the midst of Terror and Indignation was conspicuous, made her appear an Angel seiz'd by a Fiend. — Oh! if you have Honour, Generosity, or Pity, *cry'd she out, as soon as she saw* Bellcour, protect and save a wretched Maid from Violation! — His Soul, which before was so wholly taken up with admiration, now felt those Emotions she had invok'd, and presently recollecting what it was he ought to do, he drew his Sword, and bid the Villain turn and defend the Crime he was about to act, or swear he would give over all Intentions of perpetrating it, and demand forgiveness of that Excellence he had attempted to prophane. The Person to whom this Demand was made, smiled at the latter part of it with a disdainful Air, but was ready enough to answer to the former; he had his Sword out almost as soon as *Bellcour*, who leaping from his Horse, as scorning to take an unmanly Advantage, receiv'd him with equal fierceness: but the *Arm* of his Antagonist was little able to obey the Dictates of his *Heart*; he wounded him at the second or third Pass, and without receiving any hurt himself, at last disarm'd him. Now ask your Life of her whom you so impudently have sinn'd against, *said* Bellcour. — I value not my Life, *reply'd the other*; her Cruelty has made it hateful to me, and since all Means of obtaining her are ineffectual, look on Death as the only Blessing that is left me. Live then, *resumed* Bellcour, and the Curse of hopeless Love attend thee, since by such base and abhor'd Ways thou soughtest the gratification of thy Passion. He had scarce spoke

these Words, when the Person to whom they were address'd
flung sullenly away, not repenting of his purpose, but repining
that he had been depriv'd of the Power to accomplish it. Tho'
Bellcour wanted not Gallantry, and no Man in the world knew
better how to express himself on all Occasions; yet did he now
stand mute, and wanted utterance for the big Wonder of his
admiring Soul; while the fair Author of it, approaching him,
thank'd him for the Service he had done her, in terms so obliging and so full of sweetness, that it added a new Charm to her
already too powerful Beauty. — If in the wild confusion of her
Rage and Fright she was so lovely, how ravishing now must she
appear, when soft Serenity compos'd each delicate Feature, and
Joy for her Deliverance seem'd to revel in her Eyes, play'd in a
thousand dimpled Graces round her Mouth, and sent the returning Blood in rosy Blushes to her Cheeks! Aw'd, charm'd
and dazled, scarce could he reply to what she said; but Recollec-
tion at length getting the better of Surprize, he told her that he
should ever look on that Hour as the most fortunate of his whole
Life, because it had given him the Opportunity of rescuing her
Innocence: but if she thought the little he had done worthy of a
Recompence, it should be to let him know by what means she
came to be reduc'd to so great a danger. The Story, *said she*, is
too long to be related now, but if you will add to the Obligation
you have already conferr'd upon me, so far as to conduct me to
the Place where that vile Wretch was to attend me, you there,
generous Stranger, shall meet with those who better know how
to treat your Merit, than a young Maid, whose little Acquaintance with the World may well excuse the small Acknowledgments you have yet receiv'd. Ah, Madam! *cry'd he*, 'tis from
yourself alone that I should think it a glory to be prais'd; be
pleas'd to let me know who you are, and permit me sometimes
the Blessing of gazing on your Charms; I ask no other recompence for all I have done, or all that I hereafter may perhaps
endure. These last Words were accompany'd with a Sigh, and a
Look which had in it so persuasive an Eloquence, that the Lady
was sensibly affected with it, and feeling for him something in
her Heart which she already began to comprehend the meaning

130

of; I know not, *said she*, bound as I am to you by the greatest Obligation that Woman can receive, if I may promise you a Grant of the latter Part of your Request; — because, *continued she, after a little pause, and with an Air which denoted a secret Dissatisfaction*, there are Ties which leave one not the power to do as we cou'd wish. You are not married? *interrupted he, equally troubled.* The Ceremony has not pass'd, *answer'd she*, nor indeed have I yet seen my future Master; and for that reason cannot form a Judgment how far I may presume, when I hereafter shall become his Wife. *Bellcour* cou'd not here forbear looking on the Sympathy between their Fortunes, as something ominous, and immediately related to her the Destiny which was decreed for him, and that his Father was every day in expectation of the arrival of a Lady from *Jamaica*, to whom he design'd he shou'd be married. He had no sooner concluded on this Head, than the beautiful Stranger demanded hastily of him, what was the Name of his intended Bride; for, *said she*, I know many People in that Island, and may probably give you a better Account of her than you can have from any other Person. Which he making no scruple to reveal, *Mirtamene*, Madam, *said he*, is the Name of her whom my Father has made choice of for me; I have hitherto been much averse to the devoting myself, where *Duty* and not *Love* is the incitement; — perhaps, too, she may have the same Sentiments; — at least I hope so, because as I have no Heart to give, I should be sorry to receive a Present, for which I can make no valuable Return. Never did any Face discover a more visible Alteration than did that of the Lady at this Discourse; a perfect Satisfaction, almost to a degree of Rapture, smil'd on every Feature. *Bellcour* could not avoid observing it, but could not guess the Cause; and asking her if she did not think his Father too severe in the Constraint he put upon him: You have yet never seen *Mirtamene*, *said she*, and 'tis my Opinion she will appear more agreeable to you than you imagine; as for my own ease, I am willing to believe the Man design'd by Heaven for my Husband will do to me. — But, *continued she*, if you repent not of the Offer your Complaisance some moments since made me hope, I will conduct you to those

131

who are able to make you perfectly sensible what *Mirtamene* is. He then took her by the Hand, and led her to the Place where he had seen the Horses fastned, telling her as they went, that he would willingly conduct her to the farthest part of the World; and that nothing cou'd be more delightful to him, than to find she had a long Journey, that so he might not too soon be depriv'd of the Pleasure of attending her. Having set her on her Horse, and mounted himself on his own, he desir'd she would acquaint him which way (for there were two Roads) it was that she design'd to go. But she told him, she was entirely a Stranger in those Parts; but that the Name of the place which put a period to her Travels, for some time, was *Plimouth*. Nothing could be more surpriz'd than was *Bellcour* at her naming that Town; it was impossible for him to go there, without being heard of by his Father, and must therefore be oblig'd to return home: and he began to look on this Adventure, which drew him as it were whether he would or not, back to his Obedience, as if design'd by Heaven to prevent his forsaking a Father, who had always so tenderly lov'd him, that, till the Offer of Marriage which *Boanarus* had made for him with his Daughter, he had never denied him any thing his Wishes crav'd. He was so much taken up with these Cogitations, that he interrupted not the Lady, who seem'd also deeply musing in hers; and they said little more to each other, till they met some Servants whom *Maraphill*, missing his Son, had sent out in search of him, and who now attended him and his fair Charge to the Town: where being arriv'd, she ask'd of some People she saw standing in the Street, where it was that the Passengers who lately came ashore were lodged; which being inform'd of, they rode up to the House, where as soon as she alighted she was receiv'd with a Transport of Joy by a grave old Gentleman who stood at the Door. But as soon as the first Gratulations of Love and Tenderness on both sides were over; Where, *said he*, is *Clavio*, and who is this Gentleman by whom you are accompany'd? Oh, Sir, *reply'd she*, I have such a Story to relate of the Villany of that execrable Wretch, as you would scarcely credit, had I not this Witness of it. — With these Words she presented *Bellcour*. To this

generous Man, *said she*, I owe my Life, my Honour, the Pleasure of beholding you again; and in fine, every thing that's dear
and valuable to me. It is not to be doubted but that *Bellcour* now
receiv'd all the retributions that Words could yield, tho' longer
and more strenuous perhaps they would have been, had not the
Gentleman's curiosity prevailed on him to defer some part of
the Thanks he design'd to make, to another time, and made him
impatient for the Particulars of an Adventure which at present
seem'd so mysterious. Tho' nothing, *said he*, ought to be more
pleasing to me than to pay my Acknowledgments to him who
has conferr'd such Obligations on so dear a Child; yet forgive
me, Sir, if I a while give truce to my Gratitude,[67] to enquire by
what unguess'd at means she came to be so far reduc'd to stand
in need of a Defender? *Bellcour* being equally impatient to know
the Beginning, as her Father was to be satisfied of the End,
joined his Entreaties with the Commands of the other; and to
satisfy both, she began in this manner:

You know, Sir! *said she, addressing herself to her Father*, that when
the Ship cast Anchor, you being oblig'd to stay a little time to
take care of something you had on board, which you were
unwilling to commit to any other Person, I was sent on shore
before you, under the Conduct of *Clavio*; who instead of carrying me where you directed him, which I remember was to this
Inn, where now we are, (thanks to all gracious Heaven, and my
kind Protector, the generous Instrument of its benignant Care
of my Unworthiness) bore me to a Wood, whose shady Horrors
and unfrequented Wilds, soon as I entred it, struck a dread
upon my Soul, and presently did I find the Effect of my fore-
boding Thoughts. We had not travell'd above twenty Furlongs[68]
before happening to cast my Eyes upon him, I saw his Countenance so alter'd, he scarce was to be known; a death-like Pale-
ness sat upon his livid Cheek, while from his flaming Eyes a
thousand Furies darted. — I knew not what I fear'd, but yet I

---

[67]*give truce to my Gratitude* enough of; have done with his thanks (OED).

[68]*twenty Furlongs* about two and one half miles; one furlong equals an eighth of
an English mile, or 220 yards (OED).

trembled with an unspeakable Terror: Alas! it was not long before he let me know I had a dreadful Cause for apprehension; for jumping suddenly from his Horse, he took mine by the Bridle, and obliging me to dismount, Forgive me, Madam, *said he*, that I take this way, in all appearance so rough and un-courtly, to tell you the long-hid Passion of my Soul; I love you, I adore you, and as I know there is too great a disparity in our Fortunes, for me to hope to gain you by such means as Lovers ordinarily make use of, I have laid hold of this Opportunity, which your Father has given me, of telling you, that since I cannot expect to marry you, I must enjoy you; — the Possession of your Charms is a Blessing so necessary to my Peace, that I wou'd prefer Death in its most hideous Tortures, to a long Life without you. — Yield therefore with willingness to the Joys of Love, which I swear by those Powers which gave you such transcendant Charms, shall be inviolably kept secret. — A vast deal more he uttered, to the same horrid Meaning, which is needless to repeat, nor indeed have I the power to do it: Fear, Rage, Disdain, Despair, and Shame at once invaded me, and render'd me incapable of hearing, or at least remembring half of what he said; all that I know, is, my resistance being too weak to oppose his Strength, I was oblig'd to have recourse to Entreat-ies; I wept, I begg'd, I kneel'd, nay even promis'd I wou'd conceal his base Attempt from you; and if he wou'd desist, hear him urge his Suit with patience: but sooner might my weak Breath have stop'd the warring Winds, or stop'd the flying Thunder in its Course, than move the Soul of this obdurate Villain: and had not this Gentleman appear'd as my Guardian-Angel in Distress to save me, I had been the most abandoned and wretched Creature that the Sun's Eye e'er saw. Here she stop'd, and *Bellcour* perceiving the recital of this Adventure was painful to her, finish'd the History of it, by telling her Father in what manner he had resented the injury he was about to do, and his remorseless and impudent Behaviour, even after he found himself defeated. 'Tis needless to repeat the Exclamations in which they both join'd, on the monstrous Passions with which some Men suffer themselves to be agitated: after which, the old

Gentleman proceeded to tell *Bellcour* how doubly vile, from what it wou'd have been in any other Man, this attempt was in *Clavio*; for that he being the Son of a Person reduced to great misfortunes, and wholly friendless in the World, his Charity had taken him into the House, made him his Clerk, allowed him a handsome Salary for that Service, and conferr'd many other Marks of favour on him. As they were in this Discourse, a Waiter came in, and inform'd the Company that there was a Gentleman enquired for one *Boanarus*, a Merchant lately arrived from *Jamaica*: Oh 'tis my dear *Maraphill*, said he, I sent to advertise him of my coming, being told here, that he was in these Parts. In speaking these Words, he ran out to meet him, leaving *Bellcour* in a Consternation, which cannot be well express'd — to reflect that in attempting to fly his Father's House, he had met with an Adventure which oblig'd him to return on his own accord; and that the very Woman whom to avoid, he wou'd have ventur'd all things, was the Person who had induc'd him to come back, seem'd to him so strange a mystery of Fate, as took up all his Thoughts. *Mirtamene*, who imagin'd his Silence, and the deep Study she beheld him in, proceeded only from his surprize of meeting her in so unexpected a manner, and perhaps too at finding her so much more agreeable than he had figur'd her out in his mind; smiling, said to him, You see now the Reason why I did not on your first demand acquaint you who I was: by the few Words you utter'd, and the Description I had heard of you from those who have seen you, and have since been in *Jamaica*, I guess'd that you were *Bellcour*, and had a Curiosity to see how you wou'd behave to me, before you knew me to be the Daughter of *Boanarus*, and your intended Bride. Ah Madam! *reply'd he*, you cannot be so much a stranger to your unequall'd Charms, as to imagine they needed the Assistance of your Name to subdue any Heart who was not altogether unsusceptible of Beauty. — She was about to make some obliging Answer to these Words, when the two Fathers came into the Room: 'Tis hard to say, whether the Joy or Amazement of *Maraphill*, at the sight of his Son, in a Place where he so little hoped to find him, was the most predominant; or if it either exceeded that of *Boanarus*, when he found that lovely and accomplished Gentleman, whom he had been infinitely taken with before he knew him, to be *Bellcour*, was the Person to whom he had promis'd his darling Daughter. Some time was past in mutual Gratulations; after which, *Maraphill*, who was impatient to know how all this came about, was inform'd by his Son of the Truth of every thing, excepting only that he had a Design of leaving *Plymouth*, excusing himself for going into the Wood, by saying, that being too eager in the pursuit of his Game, he had out-rode his Company, and missing his way, lost hearing of the Horns.

Boanarus and his Followers having refreshed themselves after the Fatigue of their Voyage, *Maraphill* wou'd needs have them to his House, telling his old Friend, he now thought himself the happiest of Mankind; that he thought it best to have the Marriage of the young People celebrated in the Country, and that after that they would go all together to *London*. The Father of *Mirtamene* was of the same opinion, and no one at that time offered any thing in opposition to it.

Nothing now but Feasting and Mirth was to be seen in the Family of *Maraphill*; he was overjoy'd to find *Mirtamene* such as he thought it impossible his Son cou'd dislike, and that in his addresses to her, he rather appear'd as a passionate Lover, than as a Person who was to marry her on Compulsion. *Boanarus*, charm'd with the Behaviour and Perfections of his intended Son-in-Law, bless'd the happy Moment in which he made that choice. But all the Rapture that either of these was capable of knowing, was short to that which fill'd the Soul of *Mirtamene*, the moment she ow'd her deliverance to *Bellcour*; she fancy'd she saw something so graceful in his Air, that she in secret wish'd the Man design'd to be her Husband might have some resemblance of this lovely Stranger: and no sooner found he was indeed the Person, than she felt a Pleasure, which no Words can utter. In fine, never was a Passion more sincere and ardent, than that she was inspir'd with in his favour, nor never did Woman think herself more blest than she, in being the desired Bride of so seemingly meritorious a Husband. *Bellcour* was the only Person who laboured under any Inquietudes, and his were of a nature perhaps superior to what any Man on Earth but himself ever knew. — All that Resolution, which the tenderness he had borne *Alathia* had inspir'd him with, vanish'd at the sight of *Mirtamene*; and as before he was only anxious to evade marrying her, without totally disobliging his Father, his horrors now sprung from the Reflection, that he was not in a condition to become her Husband. — How did he now repent tying that irrevocable Knot! — how regret the sudden disposing himself! — a thousand times he curs'd his Passion for *Alathia*, his Unbelief that there was a Woman in the World so infinitely more worthy, as now to his chang'd Nature *Mirtamene* seem'd; — almost distracted to find how much he lov'd, how much he was belov'd, yet was incapable of enjoying the Fruits of such a mutual Passion — How blest beyond the reach of Words, (said he to himself) might I have been, in added Wealth, paternal Love, and the possession of a Creature form'd to bestow immortal Happiness; and how accurs'd has my blind Folly, my rash ungovern'd Disobedience made me! — Sometimes he was determin'd to pursue his first intentions of departing from his Father's, which he now might easily have done, being much less observ'd than he had been, and leaving a Letter behind him, which should inform his Father of the Truth of all; but he no sooner form'd this resolution, than the Idea of *Mirtamene*, all charming, all ravishing to Imagination, rose and put a stop to the Dictates of his Virtue. — At others, he swore to himself he would reveal to *Mirtamene* herself the History of his misfortune; but Love, Shame, and the Pity for those griefs which he thought such a recital would involve her in, took from him the power: Nor cou'd he, with all that strength of Reason he was master of, decide the Contest between Love and Honour.

In the mean time, he saw every thing preparing for his Nuptials, and at last in an entire readiness, yet was he still irresolute: — Never was Anguish more insupportable, more terrible, than that he endured the Night before the appointed Day; but still did his ill Genius, and the guilty Passion he had for *Mirtamene*, render it impossible for him, either by flying to escape the Crime he was so near acting, or by declaring to any

one the Truth, seek Comfort from Advice or Precept: — Sleep
had the whole Night been a Stranger to his Eyes, yet was he in
Bed, when his Father came into the Room; who reproaching
him in a jocular way, for the little Sense he had of his approaching Happiness, he only answer'd in a sullen manner, that he was
indispos'd, and wish'd the Marriage had not been so suddenly
appointed. These Words, and the Air with which they were
pronounc'd, soon chang'd the gay Humour *Maraphill* had been
in, into one wholly the reverse: he flew immediately into his
former Passions, and renewed his Curses on his Son, if he did
not instantly rise, and prepare himself to obey his Will. *Bellcour*,
to whom no shock cou'd be greater than that of his displeasure,
utter'd in terms so bitter, terrify'd with the Thoughts of incur-
ring it for ever, attended by Want, Shame, Censure and all the
Ills of Poverty, and at the same time fir'd with the Beauties of
Mirtamene ever present to his Mind, assur'd him of Compliance
to his Command: but he had not left the Room two Minutes,
before the Wrong he was about to do *Alathia*, awak'd Conscience
with so severe a Check, that he was *then* more resolute than ever,
rather to die than be guilty of so detestable a Crime. With these
Thoughts he dress'd himself, designing no other than when he
came into the Room where the Company expected him, to
relate the whole Story of his Marriage with *Alathia* before them
all. — It is better for me, (sigh'd he out) to endure all that the
Fury of an offended Father can inflict upon me, than to become
unworthy of the name of Man, by falsifying my Vows to one
that loves me. Settled in all appearance in this Disposition, he
left his Chamber; but the first Person he met, being *Mirtamene*,
the sight of her in a moment chas'd from his Soul all the Ideas
which Honour, Virtue, and the remembrance of *Alathia* had
created there; — he flew to her, embrac'd her, and in that moment of Delight despis'd all other Considerations: He led her to
her Father and his, and express'd himself in terms so full of
Transport at the Happiness they had decreed for him, that
neither of them had any reason to suspect but that he thought
himself compleatly blest. In fine, the fears of Beggary, the Desire he had to possess *Mirtamene*, together with the Reflection

that tho' he was marry'd to the other, it had been done with so much privacy, that no Person but herself had the power of declaring, and that she neither knew the Name nor Place of Abode of the Clergyman who had joined their Hands, and that since he had a Release from her own Hand from all former Ties and Obligations; made him no longer hesitate to satisfy at once his Father's Will, and the wild Cravings of his own Desires: They were married in a few hours after he had finished this Debate within himself, in the presence of as many Witnesses as the Retirement they were in cou'd produce. To the enjoyment of his criminal Transport, let us leave him for a while, and return to poor *Alathia*.

That tender and obliging Wife delayed not making all imaginable speed to Town; but how strangely was she surprized, when at her return she heard that *Maraphill* with all his Family were retir'd to *Plymouth*. But so much did she depend on the Love and Honour of *Bellcour*, that she guess'd the Thing as really it was, and made herself easy in the assurance that he wou'd on the first opportunity return. The first of her uneasiness was, that she received no Letter from him, thinking if he had retain'd those Ardors he formerly profess'd for her, industrious Love wou'd have form'd some contrivance to attest its Truth. At length the Report of his being married reached her Ears; the first Information she rejected as altogether fabulous, but hearing it confirm'd by all the Mouths which mentioned him, she began to tremble lest he had indeed been prevailed on through Interest or a new Inclination to commit that Crime: yet still unwilling to believe him base, and unable to endure uncertainty in an Affair of so much consequence, she resolved to know the Truth; and as nothing but ocular Demonstration could convince her it was so, she procur'd herself a Suit of Men's Clothes, and in all things equipt like a Youth of fashion, went in the Stage-Coach to *Plymouth*; having pretended to her Father, that she had a Desire to return to the Place she came from in the Country, and chang'd her Habit at the House of a Friend to whom her overpowering Anxieties had oblig'd her to reveal the Secret of her Marriage.

Being arriv'd at *Plymouth*, she easily inform'd herself where was the House of *Maraphill*; and going there, and enquiring with an aking Heart if *Bellcour* was at home, was told by the Servants that he was, and immediately desir'd to walk into the Parlour, where she waited not long before her perfidious Husband appear'd. *Guilt*, tho' not *Love*, brought her so frequently to his mind, that in spite of her disguise he knew her the moment he set his foot into the Room–and before she could speak to him, Oh *Alathia!* *cry'd he*, why have you done this? – I know I have been guilty of a Crime, and am sufficiently punish'd for it in unceasing Racks of Thought; – but little did I think you wou'd have join'd with my Tormentors to distract me: I am guilty, I am wretched, what more would your Revenge require? – in pity therefore leave me, nor by bringing to my sight one I have so greatly wrong'd, increase Calamities which are already too great to be supported. All that one can figure out in Imagination would come far short of that shock which struck the Soul of the amazed *Alathia* at this plain Confession of his Crime; and the Gentleness of her Nature, having never before been ruffled in so terrible a manner, must of consequence have depriv'd her of the power of resenting, or convert to a Rage equal to the injuries which excited it: what was the Effect of hers, her Actions, not Words declar'd. You shall no more be persecuted with *Alathia*, *cry'd she*, (drawing her Sword, and plunging it hastily into her Breast;) thus I deliver you from the upbraidings of an injur'd, but too tenderly loving Wife. With so much Violence she struck the Blow, that he presently in attempting to draw the fatal Weapon forth, perceiv'd it cou'd not be done without the Life-Blood issuing with it. The Cry he sent forth, brought *Mirtamene*, who was no farther than the next Room, immediately into this. What was now the Condition of *Bellcour*, let any one, if it be possible for them to do so, conceive. He saw the Woman whom he had once lov'd, with an extremity of ardor breathing her last, through his Ingratitude and Perjury: – those Eyes which had so often charm'd him, swimming in floods of Tears, more for his Guilt than the sad Consequence it had produc'd on herself, on the one side; and on the other, the deceived *Mirtamene* with, even in ignorance, Reproaches in her Eyes, for what was else the innocent Wonder she express'd at the sad Tragedy before her; was something too terrible to be withstood: he could not live and bear it, but snatching suddenly his Sword, which happened to lie on a Table in that Room, put a period to his Life by the same way his injur'd Wife had done. The Shrieks of *Mirtamene* brought *Maraphill, Boanarus*, and others who happened to be there that day, to be Witnesses of this dreadful spectacle. What *Bellcour* could not in his Life-time reveal, in the pangs of Death he declared before them all; and having ask'd forgiveness of *Mirtamene*, he turn'd to the dead Body of *Alathia*; Now, now my dear wrong'd Wife, I return for ever to thy Arms; and then expir'd. *Mirtamene* swooned away, and *Boanarus* and *Maraphill*, before half stupefied with what they saw and heard, seem'd a while to forget the Dead in the Cares of the Living. Soon did their endeavours bring her to herself, but 'twas long before she could listen to any Arguments of Consolation; and *Maraphill*, oppress'd with grief for the death of his Son, resign'd his Life in a short space after; nor did *Boanarus* long survive him. *Mirtamene*, warn'd by the example of *Bellcour*, that Interest, Absence, or a new Passion, can make the most seeming constant Lover false, took a Resolution ever to contemn and hate that betraying Sex to which she owed her Misfortune, and the Sight of such a Disaster as she had beheld in *Alathia*.

F I N I S.